Nurse Alissa vs

the Zombies

Nurse Alissa vs the Zombies

Scott M. Baker

Also by Scott M. Baker

Novels
Shattered World I: Paris
Shattered World II: Russia
The Vampire Hunters
Vampyrnomicon
Dominion
Rotter World
Rotter Nation
Rotter Apocalypse
Yeitso

Novellas
Dead Water
Nazi Ghouls From Space
Twilight of the Living Dead
This Is Why We Can't Have Nice Things During the Zombie Apocalypse

Anthologies
Cruise of the Living Dead and other Stories
Incident on Ironstone Lane and Other Horror Stories

A Schattenseite Book

Nurse Alissa vs. the Zombies
by Scott M. Baker.
Copyright © 2020. All Rights Reserved.

ISBN: 978-1-7351312-0-7

Cover Art © by Christian Bentulan 2020

To all my fans who have been asking when I'm going to start writing about zombies again.

To my colleague and dear friend Alina who kept nudging me to get back into zombies.

This series would not have happened without you.

Chapter One

ALISSA MADISON GRIMACED as she sipped her coffee. She was used to it being tepid, more often than not the coffee having sat in the pot since the beginning of the shift. This shit tasted horrible. One of the nursing students must have made it, sacrificing any semblance of flavor for the infusion of caffeine. If she continued drinking this, it would kill her and bring her back from the dead. Alissa poured the contents of her mug and what remained in the pot down the drain, washed out both, and made a new pot.

The door to the break room opened. Jaclyn Simmons, one of the other ER nurses, walked in, chatting with Doctor Michael Reynolds, the attending doctor. Jaclyn had been her friend since Alissa had moved to Boston and began working at Mass General three years ago. Both women were in their mid-thirties, although Jaclyn was flirtatious and free spirited, which Alissa attributed to her being a redhead. Dr. Reynolds recently had joined the staff, having completed his residency six months ago at Shands Hospital in Florida before taking a position here. Tall, muscular, with blonde hair and piercing blue eyes, he caused quite a sensation among the female staff.

Jaclyn stopped chatting with Reynolds long enough to watch Alissa. "We're out of coffee already?"

"I dumped the rest. That shit could have removed the rust from my car."

"How long will it be?" asked Reynolds.

Alissa finished pouring the pot of water into the coffee

maker. "A few minutes."

"We'll wait."

Alissa opened the lid. The wet filter sat inside, filled two-thirds of the way with soaked coffee grounds. She withdrew the basket and showed it to the others. "Would you look at this? Who makes coffee like that?"

Reynolds chuckled. "Someone who obviously never made it before."

Alissa stepped over to the trash can and threw out the filter, tapping the basket against the side to dislodge any loose grounds.

As she did, Stacey, one of the student nurses, strolled in. "Hey, guys."

The others acknowledged her.

"It sure is quiet tonight."

"Shit!" said Reynolds.

"Damn it!" complained Jaclyn.

Alissa dropped the basket into the coffee pot and groaned.

Stacey grew embarrassed. "What did I say?"

"Didn't they teach you anything in college?" Jaclyn asked. "You never wish someone a quiet shift."

"Why?"

"It's like the theater." Alissa did not turn her head, instead measuring out five teaspoons of coffee. "You never wish someone good luck. It jinxes you. You tell them to break a leg."

"I'm sorry." Stacey appeared as though she might cry. "I... I didn't know."

The beeper attached to Reynolds' belt went off. He slid it off, pressed the mute button, and looked at the display. "I'm needed in the ER."

Alissa closed the lid to the coffee machine and pressed the START button. "Break a leg."

Reynolds turned to Stacey and motioned to her. "You started this, so you're with me."

They rushed out of the break room, leaving Alissa and

Jaclyn alone. Alissa slid into the chair beside her friend. "I hope Reynolds doesn't rag on her too much."

"He'll put the kid to work and teach her a lesson." Jaclyn leaned closer to her friend. "What do you think of him?"

"Dr. Reynolds?"

Jaclyn nodded.

"He's a nice guy and seems competent. He'll fit in."

Jaclyn sighed good naturedly. "Do you think he's attractive?"

"Hell, yeah."

"Then why don't you hit on him?"

"Because I'm married."

"You're separated. You have been for almost a year." Jaclyn lowered her voice. "I'm not asking you to marry the guy. Find an empty room and let him rock your world for an hour."

"You're serious about this."

"Yes, I am."

"I'm not...." Alissa tried to find the right words.

"Like me?"

"That's not what I was going to say. You're single and can see who you want."

"Technically, so are you." Jaclyn held up her hand and cut off her friend in mid-protest. "Yeah, I know. You and Paul are only separated. Do you really think he's pining away for you? He's probably banging a different girl every weekend in that mountain cabin of his."

Alissa couldn't argue with her friend because, deep down, she knew Jaclyn was probably correct. Before she and Paul had gotten engaged, he had played the field, sometimes dating two or three women at once. She, on the other hand, took relationships a lot more seriously, seeing only one guy at a time. Paul had never cheated on her during the years they were married, at least as far as she knew. Now that they were separated, she would be surprised if he had not been chasing everything in a skirt. Alissa, on the other hand, approached romance and sex

3

more traditionally. Still, it had been a long time since some-one's hands other than her own had pleasured her.

"Tell you what," said Alissa. "I'll ask out Dr. Reynolds and see where it goes."

"Are you going to ask him out for coffee or dinner?'

Alissa chuckled. "What difference does it make?"

"Coffee implies you want to get to know him better. Dinner means you want to get to know him intimately."

"Fine." Alissa knew she would never win this debate. "I'll ask him out to dinner."

"Good." Jaclyn paused a moment and then grinned. "When?"

"You're not going to—"

Stacey burst into the break room, panting for breath. "We need you both down in the ER."

"What's wrong?"

"The shit hit the fan."

Chapter Two

ALISSA, JACLYN, AND Stacey rushed through the swinging double doors leading into the ER and entered total chaos. Patients occupied every room. Seven or eight stretchers lined the walls, the injured waiting for an opening. Several were strapped down, crying out in pain and thrashing about, or attacking the staff. Blood dripped from stretchers and splotched the floor. Staff had been called in from other units to deal with the crisis. A dozen police officers, including a pair of State Troopers, intermingled with the doctors and nurses, trying to keep the violent patients restrained or tend to those with the more severe wounds. A sickening stench filled the corridor, a mixture of feces, urine, sweat, blood, and decay. The noise was deafening. Doctors, nurses, police, EMTs shouted loud enough to be heard over everyone else issuing orders, yet still not enough to override the anguish of the patients.

The overwhelming sense of frustration that wracked the staff bothered Alissa most. Every medical personnel in that ER was a trained professional who had witnessed trauma running the gauntlet from car accidents to gang shootings, to the wounds caused by the Boston Marathon bombers. The atmosphere was always tense yet controlled during crises situations. Not this time. Their movements were frantic. Their voices had an edge of uncertainty when they issued commands. Desperation radiated from the staff as well as the first responders, a sense that they were struggling against a medical crisis no one had ever seen before and none of whom were prepared to cope with. For the first time in her career, Alissa watched an ER border on the brink of panic.

Stacey surged ahead, shoving her way past a stretcher against the wall where a pair of EMTs in blood-stained uniforms and Madeline, one of the newer nurses, attempted to restrain a homeless man in filthy, soiled clothes. Blood covered the man's mouth and dribbled onto his worn Army jacket. The man kicked against the wall, shoving the stretcher across the corridor and knocking Stacey against the opposite wall. The larger of the EMTs used the opportunity to push the man's left arm against the metal rim of the stretcher. Madeline grabbed the restraints and secured them around his wrist. As she did, the man lunged, biting Madeline on her left arm. She let out an agonized yelp and attempted to pull away, but the man's jaws were clenched too tight. Blood flowed around his yellowed, rotten teeth. The smaller EMT tried prying open the man's jaw to no effect. The man jerked away, tearing a chunk of flesh out of Madeline's arm. She screamed and fell against the wall, staring at the gaping wound. Madeline blanched, going into shock.

Alissa went to help but Stacey yelled to her.

"Forget them. You're needed in here."

The three nurses raced into the closest ER room.

A Boston Police officer lay on the hospital bed, breathing heavy. Blood spurted from a bite wound on his neck. A second officer stood at the head of the bed, leaning forward and firmly holding his partner against the mattress. Reynolds stood to one side, trying to stem the flow, a task made impossible by the injured trooper flailing about. Reynolds glanced up.

"Hold this guy down so I can save his life." The wavering tone to his voice made Alissa uneasy.

Alissa rushed over beside Reynolds and pushed the trooper's right arm against the mattress. Stacy and Jaclyn did the same to his left.

"What's going on?" asked Alissa.

"The fuck if I know," said the first officer. "We had a call an hour ago about a disturbance at a homeless encampment a mile from here. When we arrived, the place was like a war zone. Several of the assholes were biting everyone in sight. Some crazy, drugged up bag lady took a chunk out of John's neck."

"Where is she now?"

"Two other cops tried to take her down. I threw John in the car and brought him here."

"What if she's infected with something?"

"Worry about that later," snapped Reynolds. "This guy will bleed out if I can't cauterize the artery, and I can't do that if he's fighting me."

"I'll get some morphine." Jaclyn released the officer's arm and moved toward the medicine cabinet.

John howled. His body spasmed for several seconds and went limp. The blood gushing from his neck slowed to a trickle. Reynolds smashed his surgical instrument down on the suture tray.

"Fuck! We lost him."

Stacey released her grip on John's arm. Using her fingers, she gently slid the lids closed. Its eyes opened again, only now the orbs were milky and clouded over. It clutched the collar of Stacey's scrubs, yanked her close, and clamped its mouth over her nose and cheek. When its jaw snapped shut, teeth scraping against bone, Stacey pulled back. A huge chunk of flesh tore off, revealing the nasal cavity and upper left jaw. Stacey wiped her left hand across the wound, jumping from the pain. When she pulled her hand away, blood soaked the fingers and palm and ran down her wrist. She screamed and fell back, bumping into Jaclyn as she filled a hypodermic with morphine.

"By careful. You almost made me stab my—" Jaclyn spun around to chastise Stacey, stopping in mid-sentence.

"He bit me." Stacey gripped Jaclyn's collar with both hands, leaving a bloody handprint on the scrubs. "How bad is it?"

"Not bad," Jaclyn lied. She placed the hypodermic on the suture tray then picked up a wad of gauze from the drawer. Placing it in Stacey's left hand, she pressed it against the wound. "Apply pressure until the bleeding stops. We'll patch you up in a minute."

Everyone else stared in stunned silence at the thing that used to be John as it finished chewing on Stacey's facial tissue and swallowed. Its head jerked from side to side, seeking new prey. Upon spotting Alissa holding down its other arm, it snarled and lunged at her. Alissa knew she could not back away in time. Instead, she shoved her right forearm against the thing's neck, pushing it back onto the stretcher, and jammed her wrist into the front of its neck, lodging her hand against the chin. Clasping her knuckles with her left hand, she kept its head immobilized. The thing snarled and spit, desperate to break free and feed. Its hands clawed at Alissa's arms, trying to disrupt her grip. The other officer, who still stood at the head of the stretcher, leaned forward, seized the thing's wrists, and pinned them to the surface. Alissa knew she could not restrain it for long.

Reynolds picked up the hypodermic Jaclyn had been filling. He jabbed the needle into the thing's neck and pressed the plunger in one quick motion. The morphine had no effect.

"Try again!" Alissa yelled.

Reynolds rushed over to the medicine cabinet and refilled the hypodermic.

Alissa felt her strength weakening. "Hurry up!"

"I'm coming." Reynolds repeated the process, his hands shaking. Once finished, he withdrew the needle and stepped back a foot.

Nothing happened. The thing thrashed about even harder.

"Up the dosage!" she ordered.

"I can't." Sweat formed on the doctor's forehead and dripped down his brow.

"Why not?"

"I used the rest of the bottle. I gave him enough morphine to kill him."

Alissa felt a surge of panic mix with the adrenaline rush. "That's what I was afraid of."

"What?"

"He's already dead."

The deader rolled to its right, breaking free from Alissa's grip, and sunk its teeth into its partner's lower arm. The officer pulled away, dragging the deader with him and off the stretcher. Both hit the floor, knocking over the suture tray and strewing medical instruments everywhere. Scrambling onto its partner, the deader attacked the officer's neck, tearing out a chunk. The officer cupped the deader's head and pushed it away, three fingers on his right hand sliding into its mouth. Biting down, the deader severed them above the metacarpal joints. When the trooper yanked his hand away, the deader lunged at his neck again, biting several times in the same area. An arterial spurt of blood shot out, landing across Alissa's face.

Reynolds bent over and tried to pull the deader away. For several seconds it ignored him, concentrating instead on feeding. He wrapped his right arm around its neck, applying a choke hold to yank it away. The deader broke free and went after the doctor, dragging him to the floor. Reynolds attempted to fight it off, the futile effort ending when the deader ripped open his shirt and dug its fingers into his abdomen, puncturing the skin. The deader pulled the abdomen open, grasping a length of intestine that it unwound and shoved into its mouth, gorging on the fresh meat. Reynolds' scream turned Alissa's blood cold. She had never witnessed anyone in such agony before. The cries ended abruptly and his spasming body went limp. Alissa could not be certain if Reynolds had died or merely slipped into shock. Not that it mattered.

Alissa forced herself back to reality. The idea of tending to the sick had gone out the window when the dead started coming back to life. Putting them, and wounded, out of their misery was the best she could hope for. Moving around the stretcher, she quietly closed in on the deader, making sure not to attract attention to herself. She reached for the 9mm Glock in the deader's holster, pausing with her hand a few inches away from the grip, afraid of what would happen if she went for it. The deader finished feeding off Reynolds and lifted its head, searching for its next meal. Alissa grabbed the Glock and pulled. It stayed in the holster.

Shit, she thought. She had forgotten to unfasten the strap holding it in place.

The deader glanced over its shoulder and snarled. Alissa fell backwards. Luckily, she had not loosened her grip on the Glock, so the quick motion snapped open the fastener. When she hit the floor, she still held the weapon in her hand. The deader stood and shoved the stretcher across the room to get to her. It hissed, preparing to strike. Alissa fumbled with the weapon.

Jaclyn lifted the cart supporting the suture tray and smashed it against the back of the deader's head. It spun around to face her. Jaclyn swung it again, slamming the side of the cart into the deader's face. Shattered teeth flew across the ER and its jaw unhinged on the right, dangling at an obscene angle. When Jaclyn attempted to swing the cart again, the deader attacked, shoving the cart aside and pushing her against the wall. It bent its head to one side and bit her neck. Because of the shattered jaw, it could not break the skin. Jaclyn placed her palm on its upper jaw and pushed its head away a few inches.

"Help me!"

Alissa snapped out of her daze. Holding the Glock properly, she stepped forward to help Jaclyn. A growl sounded on her right.

The second Boston police officer had reanimated and crawled to its feet. It glared at her through milky eyes, its expression confused. Once it realized it confronted prey, the second deader snarled and charged. Alissa raised the Glock, aimed at its forehead, and fired two rounds. The first struck at an angle, having little effect other than slowing its charge. The second hit between the eyes. The hollow point crushed on impact, the metal ripping its way through the brain stem and blowing a hole the size of a fist out of the back of its head. Shards of bones, brain matter, and blood splattered across the wall. The deader collapsed.

Reynolds, now one of the living dead, had crawled over to where Stacey lay in shock in the corner and had fed off her. When Stacey died from loss of blood, Reynolds stood, seeking more food. Noticing the first deader going after Jaclyn, he stumbled forward to join the feast. Alissa wanted to conserve ammo, knowing she would need it later. She picked the scalpel off the floor with her left hand. Reynolds turned to face her. She plunged the blade into its eye and, with her right hand, pushed the handle until the instrument slid into its brain. Rather than drop to the floor, it staggered. Reynolds shook its head as if recovering from a punch and lunged. Alissa jumped back. Reynolds' intestines, hanging from its abdomen, became entangled in the stretcher. As it yanked to free itself, she stepped forward, placed the Glock three inches from its face, and fired. The hollow-tipped round shattered its head, covering her in gore.

Jaclyn screamed. Stacey had come back to life and attacked Jaclyn from behind, biting her shoulder. Jaclyn would become one of the living dead within minutes. Alissa had no time to lose. She stepped over to the officers, removed the spare magazines from their utility belts, took the second trooper's Glock, and shoved them into her scrub pockets. As she exited, she paused long enough to pump two rounds into Jaclyn's head, sparing her from a horrible afterlife.

Entering back into the corridor, Alissa gasped. What had occurred inside the room took place on a much larger scale throughout the ER. The deaders had gotten the upper hand. Half the staff and police officers from a few minutes ago were now living dead themselves, feeding off the few survivors who remained. The entrance to the waiting room stood a hundred feet away. If she moved now, she might make it. Holding the Glock in front of her, she raced down the corridor, careful not to slip on the blood covering the floor. She reached the doors without being noticed, pushed them open as she burst through into the waiting room, and stopped.

"You've got to be fucking kidding."

Chapter Three

CLOSE TO A hundred deaders packed the waiting room, with almost as many wandering through the parking lot outside. Everyone had already turned into the living dead, with no one remaining alive to serve as food, except herself. Her entrance made enough noise to attract their attention. A hundred pairs of milky eyes stared at her. With a collective snarl, the horde surged forward.

The automatic doors started to close, threatening to trap her in the waiting room. Alissa placed her free hand between the gap. She pulled open the left side enough to slip back into the ER, making it to safety as the deaders reached where she had been standing seconds ago. The mass of bodies slammed the door shut behind her, preventing them from getting in.

Her luck ended there.

The noise from the waiting room attracted the attention of those deaders in the corridor. They all turned toward the fresh prey.

An empty stretcher stained with blood stood three feet away against the wall. Alissa got behind it and ran down the corridor, using the stretcher as a battering ram. She easily pushed the first five or six deaders out of the way. Halfway down, the pack became thick and slowed her progress. She would be damned if she allowed herself to die this way. Summoning all her strength, she pushed harder and burst through. The exit on the opposite end of the ER stood only a few yards away. When she reached it, she spun the stretcher vertical across the corridor to block the deaders' advance and swiped her badge across the automatic lock. Dozens of dead hands reached for her. Both doors popped open. Alissa ran through into the main part of the hospital. A deader in shabby clothes, probably one of the homeless victims of the outbreak, bounded over the stretcher and through the doors moments before they closed. It stumbled, regained its footing, and chased after her.

Alissa broke into a full run and headed for the stairwell one hundred and fifty feet away. Damn, these deaders were fast. This one gained on her. She would have to take it out. When Alissa reached the stairs, she stopped, spun around, and raised the Glock, centering the sight on its forehead.

A ping caught Alissa's attention. The elevator to her right opened. A male nurse exited, pushing an overweight, elderly woman in a wheelchair into the corridor, directly in front of the deader. It tripped over them, knocking the poor woman onto the floor and shoving the nurse back into the elevator. The deader crawled over to the elderly woman and sunk its teeth into her left leg. Alissa expected to see blood flow from the wound. Instead, broken teeth dropped onto the floor. The woman used her cane to beat the deader on its head and back.

"Get off me."

"Are you all right, Mrs. Byrd?" The male nurse came out of the elevator, slid his hands under her armpits, and pulled the elderly woman. Her prosthetic leg broke loose, the deader still chomping on the plastic coating.

"What's wrong with that asshole?"

As if it heard the insult, the deader glared at them and hissed. Alissa stepped forward and fired a round into the back of its head, exploding its skull. Slipping the Glock into the waistband of her scrubs, she righted the wheelchair.

"Get away from me." The woman brandished the cane menacingly.

The male nurse trembled. "Please don't hurt us."

"I saved your lives." Alissa reached over to help lift the elderly woman, who smacked her shoulder with the cane. Alissa yanked it out of her hand and tossed it down the corridor.

"I'm calling security." The male nurse entered the elevator and lifted the phone out of its cradle.

"We don't have time for this shit."

The male nurse listened for a moment. There was no dial tone. He tapped the cradle several times. "Why isn't anyone answering?"

"Because they're all dead."

"Did you kill them?"

Alissa rolled her eyes. "Help me get her back into the wheelchair."

She attempted to lift the elderly woman again. This time she punched Alissa, though the blow barely hurt. "I'll call the police."

"Good luck finding one alive," Alissa snapped in frustration. "Now let me help you back into your chair before it's too late."

As if on cue, a noise emanated from the branching corridor outside the ER, the one that lead to the front lobby. Alissa held up a hand for the others to be silent and listened. She heard slow, shuffling footsteps. One or two of the deaders must have wandered in from the lobby, attracted by all the noise from a minute ago. They had a chance of getting out of this if each of them stayed calm.

"What is it?" whispered the male nurse.

"One of those things is around the corner. Let's get her back in the chair and into the elevator."

"Stop whispering behind my back." The elderly woman spoke in a loud voice.

A grunt came from the branching corridor.

Alissa placed her forefinger across her lips.

"Don't tell me to be quiet," yelled the elderly woman. "I

15

want to know what's going on."

A snarl came from around the corner, followed by the pounding of running feet. From deep inside the lobby, a chorus emanated from a pack of deaders attracted by the noise. Alissa picked up the cane from the floor and headed for the corridor.

"Get her out of here. I've got this."

Alissa brandished the cane like a baseball bat. She reached the intersection the same time as the deader and, with one violent swing, struck it on the side of its head. The deader spun around, momentarily stunned. She raised the cane above her head and brought it down on top of its skull. A loud crack echoed through the corridor and it dropped to its knees. Alissa kept up the assault. After a few more blows, the deader's skull caved in and it fell face first onto the tiles.

A dozen deaders rushed down the corridor toward Alissa, still fifty feet away. Dropping the cane, she ran back to the stairwell. The male nurse had gotten the elderly woman into the wheelchair and pulled it into the elevator, backing himself against the wall. He reached for the buttons but his hand was too far away. Pushing the elderly woman forward a few inches, he sidestepped around the wheelchair and pressed the button for another floor. In order to buy them some time, Alissa withdrew the Glock from the waistband of her scrubs and fired into the pack, the shots random and having little impact. A male deader in a blood- and gore-soaked business suit wedged itself between the closing elevator doors and pushed its way in. Several more followed. Human screams and feral noises came from inside. Alissa ignored it, moving towards the stairwell and firing until the slide locked open. She slipped the Glock back into the waistband of her scrubs, burst into the stairwell, and started up.

More than a dozen zombies chased after her.

Alissa had hoped the deaders could not climb stairs, a mistake that nearly proved fatal. They chased after her, their speed slowed only by their numbers. Alissa took the steps two at a time, gaining distance but tiring out quickly. A locked gate on the fourth-floor landing blocked the stairs to the roof. Her staff badge worked on it. If she could make it there before the deaders, she could trap them on this side. Once on the roof, she could rest and plan her next moves.

By the time Alissa reached the third floor, she still had a ten-step lead on the deaders. Her heart pounded in her chest and she found it difficult to breathe. Only one flight left. *Come on*, she told herself. *Don't give up now.* Alissa sprinted, her badge in her right hand.

When she reached the mid-way landing, a voice from above called out, "This way."

Another nurse stood on the fourth-floor landing, her back against the open gate. She held a fire extinguisher.

"Hurry. You can make it."

Alissa pushed herself, bounding up the last few stairs and practically diving through the open gate. The other nurse placed the fire extinguisher on the ground and pushed it down the steps. It had the anticipated effect. The lead deaders tripped on it, falling into a pile that blocked those behind them. During the melee, the nurse closed and secured the gate, then ushered Alissa up to the roof. She held out her hand.

"I'm Courtney."

Alissa took the hand and huffed out her name.

"Don't worry. You're safe for now."

The deaders reached the gate, shoving their hands through the bars and snarling. Alissa felt confident they would not break through.

Another voice came from farther up, this one younger. "Courtney, is she okay?"

A young girl approximately ten years old stood by the opening to the roof, wearing slip on shoes, sweatpants, and a sweatshirt. Her face lit up when she spotted the two women.

"We're fine," said Courtney.

The girl hugged Alissa, holding her close for several seconds. When she broke the hug, she offered her hand.

"I'm Stella. Welcome to sanctuary."

Chapter Four

"**S**ANCTUARY?" ALISSA ASKED.

"That's what I call it. This is where I come when I can't take it any more down there. Courtney brings me here so I can see the skyline. It's bad today, though."

For the first time, Alissa focused on Boston itself. It reminded her of a scene from a post-apocalypse movie. Black smoke billowed from half a dozen fires blazing throughout the city. Three blocks to the west, flames poured out of the windows of a four-story apartment building, engulfing the top two floors. No firefighters or equipment were present, either off battling other incidents or already overwhelmed by deaders. As she watched, the roof caved in, exploding the fourth and third floors into the streets where the debris caused nearby buildings to ignite. It was a chorus straight out of Hell—sirens, gunshots, screaming, vehicles crashing, and the ever-present sounds of the living dead. She wished she had not witnessed this.

Stella leaned her head against Alissa's arm. Alissa placed a hand on Stella's shoulder. "Thanks for saving me."

"Why wouldn't we?"

"How did you know I was on my way to the roof?"

"We didn't," explained Courtney. "We were up here when the outbreak occurred. I locked the gate but kept the door open so I could be warned of anything that approached. When I heard the living dead chasing you, I thought I might be able to help."

"You did. What are you doing up here?"

Courtney leaned over and gently pulled Stella away. "Why don't you check on that bird nest we found last night so Alissa and I can talk."

"Okay."

Courtney waited until the girl stepped out of earshot. "Sorry. I don't like talking about this around her. Stella has terminal cancer. She gets anxious if she's stuck in the room too long and loves the outdoors, so I bring her up here every day for thirty minutes. I guess the good news is she'll never be going back to the ward again."

Courtney forced a smile that did not conceal the tear running down her cheek.

Alissa understood how she felt. She gave the woman a hug, which Courtney returned. When they separated, Alissa asked, "Do you mind if I check out the area?"

"Go ahead, but you won't like what you see. It's like the seventh circle of Hell down there."

Alissa strolled over to the front of the hospital and peered over the side. Courtney had not been exaggerating. The areas in front of the lobby and ER, the parking lot, and the street beyond were jammed with deaders or the bodies of those so badly eaten they could not move once reanimated. Rivulets of blood flowed across the pavement, forming puddles that drained into the sewers. She assumed the carnage extended outward from here, by now probably blocks wide. Alissa did a quick calculation. The only way she would make it through that horde would be if she had a Department of Transportation snowplow.

Circling around to the west, Alissa studied the area between the hospital and the Charles River half a mile away. The neighborhood extended to Storrow Drive, which paralleled the river. The neighborhood seemed panicked but not overrun, and the traffic on the Longfellow and Massachusetts Avenue Bridges spanning the river still flowed. So far this seemed her best bet of getting out of the city. If she moved quickly, she hopefully would make it across without having to fight her way through those things.

The southern approaches also offered a good avenue of escape, at least for the moment. Route 93 moved at a glacial pace, but then it always did. She knew how to bypass the gridlock and get onto the Tobin Bridge, which crossed the Mystic River and headed north. Though the shortest way home it could take the longest amount of time because, as she knew from experience, the bridge could jam up without notice even at the best of times. This would be her second escape option.

The east side overlooked the parking garage, where she had to get to if she didn't want to walk home. A few dozen deaders shambled around the driveway between the two buildings and throughout the first floor of the garage. She tried to check out the other levels but could not see beyond a few feet since the walls blocked her view. She erred on the side of caution and assumed deaders were on those levels as well. Nothing roamed the top deck where the staff parked. She spotted her maroon Subaru Forester in the far corner. Moving farther to the right, she checked out the pedestrian walkway between the second floor of the hospital lobby and the parking garage. Not a deader in sight. Finally, a break. If she could make it down to the second floor and cross over into the garage, she had a good chance of making it out of Boston alive.

Alissa rejoined Courtney and Stella. The little girl forced a smile.

"I told you it was bad."

"It is." Alissa knelt in front of Stella and reassuringly rubbed her cheek. "But it's nothing to worry about. Is there another way off this roof?"

Courtney shook her head. "Just the stairwell."

"Please tell me you're kidding."

"I wish."

"What about a fire escape."

"None."

Alissa swore to herself.

"You could try the scaffolding," suggested Stella.

"What scaffolding?"

"They're doing construction work on that side of the building." Stella pointed to the end of the hospital facing the river. They've been replacing windows on the fourth floor. You could get back into the hospital that way."

Alissa patted Stella on the shoulder. "Can you do me a big favor?"

Stella beamed. "Of course."

"I need you to keep an eye on the walkway between the hospital and garage and let me know if you see any deaders."

The girl ran off.

"I think I can get us out of here," said Alissa. "If we—"

Courtney shook her head. "We're not going with you."

"What do you mean? You can't stay here."

"She's in no shape to crawl down the side of a building and try to make it to your car. Even if we did get out, then what? How long do you think she'll survive out there?"

Alissa couldn't respond. Courtney was right.

Courtney tried to comfort her. "Don't worry about us. We'll stay up here where Stella's happy."

Alissa sighed. "If I make it out, I'll send help."

"We both know that's not going to happen." Courtney said it out of resignation, not vindictiveness.

Alissa pulled the second Glock from her waistband and handed it to Courtney. "At least take this to defend yourself."

"Thank you." Courtney took the weapon, popped out the magazine, and emptied all the rounds into her hand. She slid two bullets back into the magazine, loaded it into the Glock, and slipped it between her back and the waistband of her scrubs. Cupping the top of Alissa's right hand, she poured the remaining bullets into it and gently squeezed. "This is all I need."

Alissa hugged Courtney before heading for the west side of the building, not wanting her friend to see her tears.

Chapter Five

A LISSA LEANED OVER the side of the building, studying the scaffolding and the façade. The fifth window along the fourth floor had been removed and a plastic tarpaulin taped across the opening, which would be easy enough to remove. Since the patient rooms along this corridor were vacant during the renovations, she felt pretty confident she would not crash into the room like a 1980's action hero only to be devoured by a pack of deaders. The toughest part would be getting down to that level. She had a drop of fifteen feet from the top of the roof to the wooden planks running the length of the scaffold. How difficult could it be?

Alissa sat on the parapet and swung around so her legs dangled off the side, the end of the scaffold on her right. The jump did not seem quite as simple from this angle. The only other option was down the stairwell leading here, which would be suicide. She took a deep breath, told herself everything would be okay, and pushed herself off. She landed on the catwalk with no problem. However, the momentum kept her moving forward and she toppled over the railing.

Reaching out, Alissa clutched at the metal supports, desperate to break her fall. She grabbed one of the diagonal braces with her right hand, which saved her from plummeting to her death. The weight of Alissa's body pulled her down, dragging her hand along the metal until it slammed into the juncture with the horizontal brace beneath it. She winced as pain shot through her fingers and down her arm. Alissa would have to worry about that later. Reaching out with her left hand, she took hold of one of the horizontal braces along the end of the scaffold and placed her left foot on top of the joint where they connected. The horizontal braces formed a makeshift ladder. One foot and hand at a time, she moved herself from the front of the scaffolding to the end, climbed up to the catwalk, and cautiously crawled over the guardrail.

Only then did Alissa realize how fast her heart pounded. She let herself calm down for a moment as she plotted her next move, warning herself against being overconfident. After a minute, she gingerly moved down to the tarpaulin-covered window.

Peering inside, Alissa could barely make out anything in the room. Most of the standard furnishings were covered with drop cloths to prevent them from getting dusty. She knocked on the metal frame. Nothing moved, so she tore down the covering, ready to duck out of the way if something appeared. Crawling over the sill, she entered the room. She heard some screaming and an occasional gunshot, but the sounds were muffled, coming from the floors below. For now, she was safe. It gave her time to check her wound.

Going into the bathroom, Alissa switched on the light and examined her right hand. Her palm was raw from where it slid along the metal base. She probably would have blisters by morning. There were a couple of jagged cuts, probably from scraping the palm along rusted spots. Turning the faucet on low so the noise would not attract attention, she cleaned the palm, knowing a fifty-fifty chance existed they would become infected. Once clean, Alissa dabbed the wound with paper towels, wincing at the stinging. Holding her right palm in front of her, she curled her fingers inward. The ring finger hurt, the pain running along the left side of the palm. The pinky did not move, sitting at an awkward angle with swelling around the base. She felt the length of it. Nothing seemed broken and the entire finger moved as one. She had only dislocated it. Alissa placed her left forefinger on top of the dislocated pinky and the left thumb beneath it, took a deep breath to brace herself, and snapped the finger back into place, stifling her cry of pain into a moan. It hurt and would bruise but should be okay in a few days.

Looking in the mirror for the first time, Alissa realized blood and gore covered her face and uniform. For a moment, she feared she might be infected but, if she was, she would have turned by now. Turning the water back on, she washed her face and hands, then used paper towels to wipe the chunks of brains and body matter off her scrubs. Appearing only slightly more presentable, she exited the bathroom and made her way to the door.

Alissa opened it slowly, listening for movement. Not hearing any, she peered out and scanned the corridor. Nothing. She stepped out and headed for the nurses' station, searching through it until she found a drawer of wrapping gauze. She used one to wrap around her hand and cover the scratches, holding it in place with several strips of surgical tape, and then did the same to her pinky and ring finger, using the latter as the brace. The other three rolls of gauze, two rolls of bandages, and a small pair of scissors went into the pocket with the spare rounds. Removing the Glock from the waistband of her scrubs, Alissa popped out the magazine. She refilled the magazine with the loose bullets Courtney had given her, then slid it back into the semi-automatic.

The main pharmacy was located on the first floor but she had no way to get there. However, each floor had a med room that should have penicillin and anything else she needed.

A weary, muffled voice called out from one of the rooms near the nurse's station. "Is anyone there?"

Alissa removed the Glock and held it in front of her. She followed the voice to Room 412 and hid behind the wall.

"Who are you?"

"Jim. Jim Brody." A pause. "Janet, is that you?"

Alissa stepped into the room. A middle-aged man lay in a hospital bed. An IV tube fed into his left arm and a blood pressure cuff and heart rate monitor were attached to his right. An oxygen mask covered his face. His eyes had a dull, tired expression to them but lit up when he saw Alissa. He pulled the mask from his face.

"Are you my new nurse?"

Alissa entered the room, checking to make certain they were alone. "New nurse?"

"Yeah. Something happened about fifteen minutes ago and all the doctors and nurses ran out of here. Something about an outbreak in the ER. I've been buzzing for ten minutes, but no one has answered. Are we going to be okay?"

"We?"

"Me and the other patients."

The terrible realization dawned over Alissa. She had been so preoccupied with saving her own life she had forgotten that there were patients still in the hospital who were sitting ducks when the deaders reached the upper floors. She walked over to the bed and checked Jim's vitals.

"What are you here for?"

"I had triple bypass surgery yesterday."

"How are you feeling?"

"Scared and in a lot of pain."

Alissa remained professional. "That's only natural. It's going to be awhile before you start feeling like yourself again."

Jim reached out a shaky hand and placed it over her wrist. "What about what's going on in the ER?"

"Don't worry about that," Alissa lied. "There was a bad accident on 93 with a lot of injuries, and they were all brought here. It's an all-hands-on-deck situation."

"When will they be back?" Jim wheezed.

Alissa replaced his oxygen mask and forced a smile. "Soon. Can I get you anything in the meantime?"

"I could use some morphine for the pain."

"Let me see what I can do."

Alissa patted Jim on the arm and left. Once in the corridor and out of his line of sight, she leaned against the wall and broke down, sliding down along the wall and laying her head against the surface. For the first time, she heard the steady tone of the call box at the nurse's station. The call light above every door on this side of the corridor was lit. Twenty lights, which meant twenty rooms filled with patients left to die. She had to make the final decision about their fate because she probably would be the last living person they would encounter.

Everything Alissa had learned as a nurse, every decent, human part of her soul, told her to save the patients. However, reality threw cold water on her emotions. Staying to protect them would be suicide and would do nothing more than slow their deaths by a few seconds, the amount of time it would take the deaders to strip her bones clean. Nothing could protect the bed ridden. As for the ambulatory, she could take them with her, but their chances of escaping from the deaders were less than if they stayed in their rooms and waited for help to arrive. Even if by some miracle she could save these twenty patients, what about those in the other wings on this floor, or the two floors below. Alissa sobbed as the truth struck home with a cruel harshness. Unless this outbreak could be contained and eradicated within twenty-four hours, which seemed highly unlikely based on what she had witnessed, most of these patients were as good as dead.

A woman's scream and the muffled sounds of snarling echoed through the elevator shaft across from the nurse's station, snapping Alissa back to the present. She came here for a reason, as selfish as it might be, and could not allow herself to be sidetracked if she hoped to live through the next hour. Standing up, she headed back to the nurses' station, ignoring the voices that called to her from each room she passed. Having any contact with them would only make it harder to carry through with her decision. When she reached the med room, she searched for her badge to unlock the electronic latch. Fuck! She lost her badge. Alissa searched on the station desk, moving papers and checking the stackable letter trays, hoping one of the nurses or doctors had left theirs behind. Nothing. One by one, she pulled open the drawers and rummaged through each. In the fifth one, she found an ID card attached to a lanyard and flipped it over. A young, smiling, blonde stared back. Patricia Menninger. If the charge nurse had caught Patricia leaving her badge unattended, she would have written her up.

Returning to the med room, Alissa swiped the badge, giving her access. She emptied the dispenser containing penicillin, popping two pills into her mouth and forcing them down without water, then took the dispenser of Percocet, figuring she would need those for her finger later tonight. She slid the bottles into her scrub's pocket beside the gauze. As Alissa headed out, she paused. Going back inside, she picked up two more items before leaving.

Alissa closed the door to each hospital room as she passed, offering the patients inside some level of protection from the deaders, no matter how minimal. Each called to her and begged for help, but she ignored them, refusing to make any connection. After all the rooms were secure, she backtracked to Room 412.

Jim broke into a smile when Alissa entered and removed his oxygen mask. "You came back?"

"I told you I would." She held up a bottle or morphine. "Let's take care of your pain."

Facing the window so Jim could not see, Alissa inserted a syringe into the bottle and filled it with one milliliter of morphine. She inserted the needle into the injection port of Jim's IV system and pressed the plunger, not stopping until she dispensed the entire amount. Alissa removed the needle and placed it on the nightstand.

"You should feel better soon."

"Thank you."

"You're welcome." Alissa replaced his mask and gently stroked his forehead.

The effects of the morphine were immediate. Jim closed his eyes and slipped into a peaceful slumber. His vital signs slowed, his blood pressure and heart rate dropping until the warning signal on the monitor blared. Alissa stopped stroking Jim and shut off the monitor. She pulled the covers over his face and rushed out.

Chapter Six

ALISSA HEADED FOR the stairwell at the rear of the hospital, the one farthest from the lobby. The chances were greater that the deaders had not reached there yet. At least she prayed they had not. She removed the Glock from the waistband of her scrubs and held it in her right hand, a task made more difficult by her pinky and ring fingers being bandaged. She peered through the small window, twisting her head from side to side, not seeing any deaders. Opening the door a few inches, she listened for several seconds for the sound of anything not human. The only noises came from deep within the building. She stepped onto the landing, closed the door slowly so it made no sound, and proceeded down.

As Alissa turned the bend in the stairs above the second-floor landing, a male figure in a white lab coat leaned against the wall, holding the right side of his abdomen and panting for breath. Blood stained the front of his lab coat and trousers. He made eye contact as Alissa raised the Glock

"Put the gun down. I'm human."

Alissa lowered the barrel. "Where did all that blood come from?"

The doctor pulled aside his right hand, revealing a gaping wound. Teeth marks were visible along the edges. A portion of his intestines had been chewed open, allowing fluid and fecal matter to drip out. The intestines began to slip out of the wound until the doctor pushed them back in.

Alissa raised the Glock and aimed at his head.

"Stop being trigger happy. I'm not going to turn."

"Yes, you are. Within a few minutes you'll become one of those things."

"I doubt it."

"Why?"

"Because I got bit fifteen minutes ago. If I was going to turn, I would have done so by now. And I'm not feeling any symptoms of the virus." The doctor winced. "Put that gun down before you kill me. I need your help."

Alissa thought about her response long enough for it to be noticeable.

"Don't worry," the doctor said in a condescending tone. "I'm not going to ask you to save my life. I wouldn't want to put you out. I need you to help me take some blood samples."

"That's not what—"

The doctor brushed her off. "If you're going to help, let's do this before I bleed out."

Without waiting for a response, he opened the door and limped into the corridor. Alissa followed, propping it open with her back as she scanned the area for deaders. When she didn't see any, she joined the doctor, placing his left arm over her shoulder and helping him walk.

"Where are we going?"

"There's a pathology lab down on the left." He motioned with his head.

Once at the lab, the doctor punched a six-digit code into the keypad. The lock opened with an electronic click. The doctor pushed his way inside. Alissa stopped to close the door manually so it would not slam shut. As she did, the doctor stumbled over to a stool by the elevated work bench and lifted himself onto it with a moan.

"By the way, I'm Doctor Edwards."

"I'm Alissa." She forewent any pleasantries and searched for syringes and needles. "How many vials of blood do you need?"

"Four." He opened a drawer on the workbench, removed a notebook and pen, opened it to blank page, and began taking notes.

Alissa removed the vials from the bin on the counter. "Where are the needles?"

Edwards pointed with his pencil. "Second drawer down."

Alissa opened it. Only rubber gloves were inside. She pulled out a pair and tossed them on the counter.

"They're not in here."

"Next one." Edwards made no effort to hide his frustration.

She found a pile of needles, alcohol rubbing pads, gauze, and tape. Taking one of each, she went back to the doctor, ripped open the plastic wrapping on the needle, and inserted it into the first vial.

"What are you writing?"

"I'm taking notes on my condition."

"Your intestinal wound?"

"That I was bitten by one of those things and haven't turned. Maybe it'll mean something later. Maybe not. But it's better than sitting around here waiting to die."

Alissa agreed. She slipped on the rubber gloves. "You'll have to stop writing if you want me to take your blood. Give me your arm."

Edwards placed down the pen and held out his right arm. Alissa wrapped the latex band around his upper arm and tied it tight. None of the veins were visible beneath the skin. She slapped the length of his arm, hoping to bring some to the surface, without success.

"Let me see your other arm."

Edwards shifted his chair to face Alissa and held out his left arm. She examined it, slapping the skin several times, and could find no veins in this one either.

"I was afraid of this."

"Afraid of what?"

"You've lost so much blood there's little left in your extremities." Alissa loosened the latex band and pulled it off his arm. "I'm going to have to get closer to where your blood now is. Pull your pants down."

Edwards managed a chuckle. "I don't think I'm up for that right now."

Unbuckling his belt and unzipping his fly, the doctor slid his pants down to his knees, exposing his groin. Blood covered his left leg. Alissa moved to the other leg, tied the latex band above his knee, and slapped the skin. Several good-sized veins emerged. Unwrapping one of the alcohol pads, she wiped the skin then removed the plastic covering from the syringe, placed the needle against the skin, and inserted. Blood spurted into the vial for several seconds before the flow slowed to a trickle. With her other hand, Alissa massaged the leg below the injection point until blood filled the vial halfway.

"That's enough," said Edwards. "Get three more samples before it's too late."

Alissa switched out the vials, being careful to place the first one against the notebook so it did not roll off the countertop. Each vial took longer to fill than the last. She could feel his pulse racing at one hundred and fifteen beats per minute, and his breathing had become fast and shallow. Alissa checked her watch. She had been here for almost twenty minutes.

With the last vial filled with as much blood as she could draw, Alissa slid the needle out of his vein and removed the vial. "What now?"

Edwards had dozed off. Alissa shook his chest.

Edwards' eyes opened. His gaze darted around the room, unfocused. "Where am I?"

"We're in the pathology lab."

He lowered his head. "Do I know you?"

"You asked me to draw blood from you."

"That's... right."

"Snap out of it." Alissa tapped him on each cheek. "You have to tell me what to do with these vials."

"Vials?"

"Of blood."

Edwards started to doze off.

"Snap out of it." Alissa slapped him across the cheek, this time much harder.

"What?"

"What do you want me to do with the blood samples?"

"You finished taking them?"

"Yes." She pointed to the four vials on the countertop.

The doctor forced himself to break through the confusion. "Put two in the freezer."

Alissa carried two of the vials to the refrigerator, opened the freezer door, and placed them into the tray where she had originally found them.

"What do you want me to do with the last two?"

"Take… with… you."

"What do I do with them?"

"You'll… know… when…." Edwards' words trailed off as the loss of blood finally took its toll. The doctor's body went limp and collapsed off the chair, hitting the floor with a loud thud.

Alissa cringed, waiting for the sound of running deaders approaching. The corridor remained silent. Only then did she realize she had been holding her breath the last few seconds.

Searching through the lockers, Alissa found two lab coats that she draped over Edwards' head and torso, providing him what little dignity she could. Rummaging through the last few, she came across a large, over-the-shoulder leather bag. She dumped the contents onto the counter and placed the rolled-up gauze, tape, penicillin, and scissors in the bag. She kept the spare ammunition in her pocket for easy access. Inside one of the cabinets she discovered a transportation container for the blood samples—a tube four inches in diameter and eight inches in length. Removing the top, she placed the two vials into the holes carved into the foam rubber interior, slid the cover back on, and added it to the other items in the bag. Moving over to the door, Alissa peered through the glass but did not see anything in the corridor. Hefting the bag over her left shoulder and holding the Glock in her right, she exited the lab.

Alissa raced down the corridor, heading for the second floor of the front lobby and the ramp to the garage. With luck, she would be safe in a few minutes.

A knocking on the right startled Alissa. She jumped back against the wall and aimed the Glock, quickly lowering it when she realized the source posed no threat.

"I can't believe this is happening," she muttered.

Chapter Seven

"CAN YOU HELP us?"

The question came from her friend Marjorie, one of the older nurses. Marjorie stood on the other side of the viewing window of the nursery. Alissa pointed to the entrance to the Labor and Delivery Department twenty feet down the corridor. She waited for Marjorie to make it there and usher her inside. Marjorie closed and locked the door behind her. Spinning around, she gave Alissa a hug.

"I'm so glad someone else is alive."

Alissa patted her back in a gesture of support. "How much do you know about what's going on downstairs?"

Marjorie broke the hug and stepped back. "Something bad happened in the ER and we've been told to shelter in place until someone comes for us. What do you know about it?"

"Not much more than you do," Alissa lied.

"You're covered in blood and holding a gun. Now do you want to be honest?"

"Sorry." Alissa sighed. "I didn't want to scare you."

"Everyone up here is already terrified."

"Something broke out in the ER forty-five minutes ago. I don't know if it's a virus or what, but it causes anyone infected to go violently insane and attack those around them. The first floor of the hospital has become a bloodbath."

"When will the police be here?"

"They're already here, and they've been turned. I tried calling for help, but all the landlines are down. My cell phone is in my car."

"It won't work. We have ours. Circuits are busy." Marjorie studied the bag Alissa held over her shoulder. "You're trying to get out of the hospital, aren't you?"

"Do you blame me?"

"Can you take the babies with you?"

The question caught Alissa off guard. "You realize how dangerous it is out there?"

"Is it any safer in here waiting for whatever's going on to reach us?"

Alissa couldn't argue that point. "How many babies are there?"

"Four."

"I can't carry four babies at once."

"We'll go with you. Only one of the mothers is still bed-ridden, but we can wheel her out in a chair."

"No!"

Marjorie became angry. "You won't help us?"

"It's not that I don't want to. Those things are fast. We'll never get the mothers past them. They'll be torn to shreds."

"You're right." The anger drained from Marjorie. She walked away from Alissa, stopping in front of the reception desk. She then kicked it so hard her foot shattered the wooden façade. "Shit!"

Alissa rushed over and pulled Marjorie back from the desk. "Keep it down. They're attracted to noise."

"Sorry." Marjorie's eyes welled up. "I can't leave everyone here to die."

"Under the circumstances, you're all safer here—"

"What if we take out only the babies?"

Alissa stared at Marjorie.

"I'm serious. There's a shuttle van parked out front. If we could make it to—"

"Those things are all over the parking lot. You'll never get that far."

"Is the parking garage open?"

Alissa nodded. "That's where I'm heading."

"Good. I have an SUV on the third level. We can escape in that."

"Why are you so adamant about taking the kids out into this carnage?"

Marjorie inhaled deeply to steady her nerves. "The mothers are freaking out. They want their kids in a safe location. Now they're freaking out my nurses. If I don't do something, they'll probably walk out of here with their babies."

"And into a slaughterhouse."

"I know." Marjorie swallowed hard, fighting back anger and frustration. "What else can I do? Help us get to the garage and I won't bother you after that. I promise."

Everything in Alissa's gut told her this would end badly. "Is there any way I can talk you out of this?"

Marjorie shook her head.

"Give me a minute to scout out the situation and I'll be back."

Marjorie held her wrist. "Promise you won't leave us?"

"If I do, you'll wind up doing something stupid." Alissa handed Marjorie her bag with the medical supplies. "I'll be back in a minute."

Leaving Labor and Delivery, Alissa made her way down the corridor to the entrance to the second-floor lobby. Approaching from an angle so she could not be seen, she peered through the window. At least a hundred deaders shunted around the main lobby, with another half dozen on the second-floor landing. The feeding frenzy had died down and now the deaders milled about. She would never slip past this horde and get to the garage, let alone four nurses laden-down with screaming infants. She needed to figure out a way to distract these things. An idea came to mind. It was a long shot and probably wouldn't work, but she had nothing else.

Once back at Labor and Delivery, Marjorie let her in.

Three other nurses stood in the lobby, two of them holding a pair of babies.

"Do you have a battery-operated radio in here?"

Marjorie shook her head.

"What about a cell phone, especially one with an alarm or music on it?"

"I might have one." One of the nurses, a young woman with auburn hair, handed one of the babies to Marjorie, reached into the pocket of her scrubs, and withdrew a cell-phone. "What do you need?"

"Something loud and obnoxious."

"I got just the thing." With her free hand, the woman un-locked her cell phone, scrolled through several apps, and handed the phone to Alissa. "It's an emergency alarm. Press the red button and everything within a mile radius will hear it."

"What's your name?"

"Carrie."

"Carrie, this is perfect." Alissa stepped around the recep-tionist desk, rolled the chair into the lobby, and stopped. "Okay, this is what we're going to do. You stay here by the exit. I'll create a distraction. Once I give you the signal, head for the second-floor lobby and take the connecting walkway into the garage."

"What about those things?" asked Marjorie.

"When I checked a few minutes ago, there weren't any in the garage. Head for your cars and haul ass out of here. Clear?"

Three of the nurses agreed. The fourth said, "I'll lock things up after you and take care of the mothers."

The four of them made their goodbyes until Alissa inter-rupted them. "We don't have time for this. Be ready to go in less than a minute."

Stepping back into the corridor with the chair, Alissa moved over to the elevator and pressed the call button. She would set the alarm, send the car back down to the first floor, and make a break via the lobby as—

A ping announced the arrival of the elevator. As the doors slid open, Alissa reached down to press the alarm button. A snarl distracted her. Fuck, she had forgotten this was the elevator where the deaders attacked the elderly woman in the wheelchair and the male nurse. Five deaders were inside, four of them mobile. They lunged.

Alissa shoved the desk chair against the pack and pushed, knocking three of them back inside the elevator. They tumbled over the elderly woman and her wheelchair, momentarily not a threat. The fourth deader, the male nurse, had not been in the path of the chair and attacked from the left. She lodged her left arm under its chin and shoved it back against the wall, holding its head in place so it couldn't bite her. With her right hand, she felt for the Glock. Her hand brushed against the grip, knocking it out of the waistband of her scrubs. She tried to reach out with her foot and draw it closer, pushing it farther away in the process.

"Move!"

Carrie came up on their left, gripping a coat rack like a battering ram. Alissa jumped back and crouched to the right a moment before Carrie drove the rack into the deader nurse's head, knocking it over. Standing above it, she repeatedly slammed the base of the coat rack against its skull. On the third hit, the bones cracked. On the sixth, the head exploded, spewing blood and brain matter down the corridor.

A snarl from behind made the two women spin around. The other three deaders had climbed to their feet and were exiting the elevator. Carrie lowered the coat rack and charged, catching a deader dressed in a soiled business suit under its chin and propelling it back into the car.

"Hurry up and finish what you have to do."

Alissa did not need to be told twice. She pressed the alarm button. A deafening noise echoed through the hospital, causing her to wince. It would attract every deader in the building.

Tossing the phone into the elevator, she leaned in and searched for the first-floor button. The deader in the business suit reached out, grabbing her arm. Being at an awkward angle, Alissa could not break its grip. It lowered its mouth. Before it could bite, Carrie slammed the coat rack into its face, shattering several of its teeth. When the deader let go of Alissa, she pressed the button for the first floor and jumped back. Carrie followed. The elevator doors began to close.

And stopped halfway.

"What the—" Alissa's sentence trailed off. The elderly deader attempted to crawl through the gap, biting at Carrie's legs. The elevator kept closing on the deader, sliding back, and closing again. Alissa heard deaders banging on the elevator doors on the first floor and at the door to the second-floor lobby, attracted by the alarm. This cluster fuck would get them all killed.

Carrie prodded at the other three with the coat rack but could not keep them at bay much longer. "Move that bitch before I get bitten."

Alissa grasped the elderly deader by the back of its gown and yanked, trying to pull it out into the corridor so the elevator would close. The living dead thing moved about a foot and stopped. Its leg had become entangled in the wheelchair. Alissa rocked its bulk back and forth while simultaneously yanking, hoping to break it lose. All the while, the elderly deader moved its head from side to side, its mouth snapping at her hands.

"Shit!" yelled Carrie as she stepped back. The top of the coat rack snapped off, gouging the face of a deader in a policeman's uniform. A deader in homeless clothes came after her, only to get the broken end of the coat rack jabbed into its eye socket. Carrie twirled it around for a moment until the deader went limp, the weight of its body pulling it off the rack and onto the wheelchair, which freed the elderly deader's leg. Alissa fell backwards, yanking the elderly deader into the corridor. The elevator doors finally closed and the car descended to the first floor. Alissa did not hear the elevator open or the feeding frenzy as the deaders rushed in to devour the alarm. She was too busy fighting for her life.

Once free of the wheelchair, the deader scrambled after Alissa. It clutched her right leg and pulled itself onto her. Alissa kicked it in the face with her left foot, slowing it but not breaking the grip. She kept on kicking, ripping off its nose and caving in the upper jaw, but still not stopping it. Its attack ceased only when Carrie spun the coat rack and plunged the broken end into the deader's skull. The thing shuddered for a moment, the snarl becoming a gurgle, and then collapsed onto Alissa's legs. She shoved the carcass out of the way and jumped to her feet, shaking from fear.

Carrie came over to comfort Alissa. "Are you okay? Did it bite you?"

"I'm fine. Thanks for saving my life."

"Let's get moving while we have a chance."

Both women ran back into the Labor and Delivery lobby. Alissa picked up her bag, only then stopping to catch her breath.

"What now?" asked Marjorie.

Alissa held up a finger, asking for a second. Once she could inhale, she replied, "I'll head down to the second-floor lobby and check it out. I'll signal you when the coast is clear, then you all make a break for your cars. Understood?"

Marjorie and the other two nurses carrying babies responded in the affirmative, although the fear in their eyes belied their outward confidence. Alissa could relate. At this moment, it would not take much to send any of them over the edge.

Exiting Labor and Delivery, Alissa rushed down the corridor, hugging the opposite wall so nothing on the other side of the lobby door could spot her. Reaching it, she leaned to one side and peered through the pane. Every deader in the main lobby swarmed toward the corridor off the ER, chasing the alarm. Most from the second floor joined the others, rushing down the stairs and escalators to follow the feeding frenzy, leaving behind a single deader in a tattered EMT uniform that limped on the side of its right foot, the ankle obviously broken. Escaping should be simple. She turned around. Carrie waited by the entrance to Labor and Delivery. Alissa lifted her arm and motioned for the others to join her. Carrie stepped aside and began ushering the nurses carrying the infants into the corridor.

Alissa heard a distinct sound, one that sickened her stomach with the realization of what would happen next.

The elevator pinged as it reached the second floor.

With all the deaders rushing in to get at the alarm, one must have inadvertently pressed the UP button. Carrie shoved Marjorie back into Labor and Delivery. The elevator opened. Knowing she would never make it to safety in time, Carrie attempted to close and lock the door from the outside as ten deaders flowed out. The first three dove onto Carrie, one clutching her head and shoulder and sinking its teeth into her neck, the other two tackling her around the waist. They fell against the door, pushing it open. The remaining deaders snarled and rushed into the unit. Alissa started down the corridor to save the others, but the terrified screams of the nurses, the crying infants, and the feral sounds coming from the living dead told her it was already too late.

Pushing through into the second-floor lobby, Alissa dropped to her knees and puked.

Chapter Eight

ALISSA RETCHED UNTIL nothing came out, then dry heaved. Her throat felt on fire. She spit out the last of the vomitus and wiped the back of her hand across her mouth. Only then did she realize she still held the Glock. Alissa stared at it. It would be so easy to end this nightmare. Quick and simple. No more suffering. No more watching others being slaughtered. No more desperate attempts to survive against the odds.

Alissa slid the barrel between her lips and placed it against the roof of her mouth when a growl came from her right. The limping EMT deader staggered toward her, its arms outstretched, its gore-filled mouth already gaping in anticipation of its next meal.

"Fuck you!"

Alissa stood and fired a shot directly into the deader's face. Its features collapsed as the back of its skull blasted across the lobby. It collapsed in front of her, twitching. She stood over it and emptied the rest of the magazine into the remains of its head and its chest. When the slide finally stuck in the open position, nothing remained of the deader above its chest other than a pool of gore.

The noise attracted the attention of a dozen deaders heading for the elevator. Spinning around, they rushed the stairs. Rather than seek safety, Alissa ejected the empty magazine from her Glock, dropped it into her pocket, and removed a loaded one. She slid the magazine into the weapon and pulled back the slide as the first deader reached the down escalator, scrambling up each step but going nowhere. Alissa concentrated on the three racing up the stairs, centering the sight on their faces, consumed by hatred. Each time a bullet impacted into dead flesh she felt a sense of satisfaction. She expended an entire magazine taking them down. It had the desired effect, slowing the ones in the back, forcing them to climb over the carcasses. Alissa switched out the magazines, this time taking more careful aim, taking out seven more before the slide stuck open. The last deader, a burly thing wearing the torn uniform of one of the hospital valets, circled around the pile of bodies and jumped onto the up escalator, bounding up the moving steps. With her fury partially satiated, Alissa's lust for revenge gave way to an instinct for survival. Knowing she could not reload in enough time to stop the last deader, she darted down the elevated walkway and ran for the garage.

Alissa approached the glass doors to the garage, studying the area ahead of her. No deaders were within eyeshot, although the corpse of a half-eaten EMT lay on the cement. Only then did Alissa realize she had miscalculated her escape. The doors were automatic and opened at the approach of a moving object. While that feature would be helpful in allowing her to escape, it would also allow the deader to follow. She had only one chance. Mustering her energy, she sprinted for the exit, putting a few extra feet between her and the deader. A click sounded and they opened. Alissa ran through the gap, spun around, and slammed them shut. At least, she tried to. Being on mechanical hinges, they resisted the change in direction. She pressed her weight against the rims, urging them to move. Finally, the mechanism shifted into reverse and they closed.

Not before the deader shoved its hand through the gap. It reached for her, trying to bite her through the opening. Alissa slammed the door repeatedly on its arm but, being unable to feel pain, it did not react. It clutched for her throat, desperate to dig into flesh and devour its prey. Instead, its fingers wrapped around the handle of her bag. With a yank, it drew Alissa closer to its gore-encrusted teeth. She inhaled its foul breath and the stench of chewed flesh and organs, wanting to puke again. Dropping her left shoulder, she allowed the handle to slide off and down her arm. The valet deader fell backwards, still holding the bag, and tumbled to the floor. Alissa ran over to the EMT, placed her Glock on the cement, removed its belt, and rushed back to wrap it around the handles. She finished securing the buckle as the valet deader slammed into the glass. The thing clawed at her, leaving streaks of blood along the pane. Alissa backed away, keeping a wary eye on it, hoping the belt would hold it back. It pushed against the glass and snarled furiously but did not break through.

Alissa backed away until something touched her back. She cried out and jumped forward, turning to face the new threat, breathing a sigh of relief upon discovering she had bumped against the railing of the stairwell. The scare snapped her back into reality. She needed to get to her car on the fifth level before all the noise attracted other deaders. Going over to the EMT, she retrieved the Glock, switched out the empty magazine and cocked the slide, loading a round into the chamber, and headed up to the next level. She slowed at the midway landing, raising the weapon and climbing one step at a time, scanning the area for deaders. A few wandered aimlessly through the parking garage, paying no attention to her. Alissa tip-toed around to the stairs leading to the fourth level, following the same procedure until she reached the top floor. Hugging the wall, she moved toward the garage, ready to use the Glock if necessary.

No deaders were visible on this level. Still, Alissa refused to throw caution to the wind. She broke right toward her Subaru, walking down the center of the lane so nothing could jump out from between vehicles and surprise her. Alissa reached her Subaru Forester, unlocked the car, and slid into the front seat, placing the Glock on the passenger's seat. She inserted the key into the ignition.

At that moment, all the pent up the emotions of the last hour gushed to the surface. Alissa laid her head against the steering wheel and cried.

Chapter Nine

A LISSA AWOKE WITH a start. She scanned the area around the Subaru for deaders as she reached for the Glock on the passenger's seat. Her heart pounded as she aimed in every direction. It took a few moments to realize nothing threatened her. She had merely dozed off, although she had no idea how long she had been asleep. It could not have been more than a few minutes, fifteen at most. The nap had done her good. Alissa felt a little more at ease and had time to think rather than react.

Reaching over, she opened the glove compartment, took out her cell phone, and pressed the power button. It took several seconds before a series of pings echoed from the device. She punched in her four-digit passcode, wondering who had texted her. It turned out no one had. She had received over a dozen warnings about road closures and the civil disturbance in Boston. Alissa chuckled. A civil disturbance? They were experiencing a fucking apocalypse. Deleting the warnings, she attempted to text her neighbor to see what things were like on Nahant. Hitting SEND, a red warning box popped up stating the message could not be delivered. Three more text attempts failed. Alissa tried to call her neighbor only to have a recorded female voice announce that all circuits were busy and suggest she try her call again later. Not that it surprised her.

Alissa climbed out of the car. Blood and gore stained the driver's seat, reminding her she looked the same way. Moving to the back of the vehicle, she raised the hatch. A backpack lay in the corner against the rear seats. Reaching in, she pulled it toward her. Paul, the amateur survivalist, had given it to her three years ago, insisting she always keep it in the Subaru. He called it a bug-out bag. Alissa referred to it as her snowbound bag, figuring she would only use it if she got stuck driving home in a blizzard. Who figured he would be right?

Unzipping the bag, Alissa emptied the contents onto the deck. It contained a change of clothes, which she desperately needed, a pair of waterproof hiking boots, and a camouflaged baseball cap. A pair of military-style tactical gloves. A small thermal blanket rolled into a bag six inches long by four inches in circumference which, according to the label, would keep her warm at temperatures above zero degrees Fahrenheit. A first-aid kit. An MTech fourteen-inch hunting knife with leather sheath. A box of matches. Three bottles of water. A bottle of multi-vitamins. And five multi-grain granola bars. Alissa opened the first-aid kit, expecting to find band-aids and aspirin, and pleasantly surprised to find it stocked with stitching needle and thread, a small bottle of alcohol, a tube of antibiotic cream, a roll of gauze, and other items.

Shit! When she let go of the bag to escape from the deader in the garage, she lost the gauze for her hands, the penicillin pills, and the two vials of blood. She reminded herself to pick up more of the first two or, better yet, see a doctor once she got out of Boston.

Alissa placed the cell phone into the outer pocket of the backpack and slipped out of her soiled clothes and shoes, putting on the clean items Paul had stored. The jeans were a little loose and the red flannel shirt baggy, which made her smile. At least she had lost some weight in the past three years. Opening one of the bottles of water, she drank half and poured the rest onto an unsoiled portion of her scrubs, rubbing down her face. When done, she crouched and checked herself in the side mirror of the Subaru. The change of outfit and clean up helped. Except for her hair, which had streaks of blood and a few chunks of gore in it, she was presentable. As she untied her ponytail, she discovered that blood had soaked the scrunchy, so she would have to let her hair down for a while. Using the wet portion of the scrubs, she cleaned her hair as best she could. A shower would be necessary to get out the rest. At least being brunette the stains were not as noticeable.

She removed the remaining three extra three magazines from her scrubs and tossed the soiled clothes against the garage wall. Her killing spree at the escalators had wasted two full magazines. What a dumb move. She chastised herself and resolved to be more careful. God only knew how much ammunition she would need to get out of Boston. She slid the weapon into the waistband of her jeans and the magazines into her left pocket. She attached the hunting knife to her belt and strapped the sheath to her right leg, then tossed the pack onto the rear passenger seat. If Paul could see her now.

Alissa bent her pinky and ring finger, rating the pain a level five, but at least she could still use it. The bandages were blood soaked; nothing she could do about that. At the first opportunity she would swing by a CVS or Rite Aid and stock up on medical supplies.

What to do now? Getting out of Boston was the priority, especially with this infection spreading more rapidly than expected. Ideally, she could make her way to the cabin in New Hampshire. It provided the perfect location to wait out the outbreak—isolated, well stocked with food, and had a secret stash of weapons and ammo for the apocalypse that Paul always told her would happen. Once there, she....

Shit! She almost forgot about Archer. He was home alone and had no way to fend for himself. She lived in Nahant, north of Boston, so the detour would not take long. With luck, they would be in New Hampshire by midnight.

A commotion on the Longfellow and Massachusetts Avenue Bridges spanning the Charles River warned Alissa that estimate would probably change. She rushed to the side of the garage overlooking the river. Cambridge Police and State troopers had set up roadblocks along the structures, preventing anyone from leaving Boston and stopping the infection from spreading. Vehicles packed the bridges, the gridlock extending to Storrow Drive. Hundreds of people had abandoned their cars and stormed the barricade, trying to escape on foot. Most ignored the police and tried to break through. The police fired a volley of warning shots over their heads. When that did not stop the rush, they fired into the crowds. Men, women, and even children were being cut down by the gunfire. The situation spiraled out of control. Even worse, the deaders rushed toward the noise, approaching the Boston side of the bridges and feeding on those near the rear of the mob. Within a few minutes, the number of living dead would be too much for the police to handle.

To her right, the same situation occurred on the road by the Museum of Science and on I-93 heading north. Police had set up roadblocks. Nothing moved. She assumed the same took place all around the city. The authorities must have decided to isolate Boston in the hopes the infection could be contained and would burn itself out. They were sacrificing the entire city. She had to move now or she would be trapped in a killing zo—

A tanker truck turning on the road to the Museum of Science exploded, probably ignited by the police shooting into the crowd. Flames shot out everywhere, incinerating dozens of people close to the tanker. Others ran away engulfed in fire, collapsing onto the road as their tissue and muscles burned. A few good Samaritans tried to douse them with their jackets, only to succumb to the burning river of gasoline flowing down Storrow Drive. As the gasoline spread, it ignited other vehicles, including a packed Metro bus. Alissa felt the bile rise in her stomach as she heard the screams of those trapped inside being burnt alive. A few seconds later, the bus and several enflamed cars exploded.

The concussion from the blast rocked the garage. The car

alarm of a BMW parked a few spaces away went off, the high-pitched noise echoing throughout the garage. From the lower levels, snarling and the thumping of feet on cement warned that deaders were racing toward the noise.

Spinning around, Alissa ran for her SUV.

Chapter Ten

ALISSA REACHED THE Forester and slid into the front seat as a dozen deaders swarmed around the corner and lunged at the BMW. She closed the door and started the ignition. The deaders turned their attention from the car and rushed her. Shifting into drive and slamming her foot on the accelerator, she barreled out of the parking space, scraping the fender of the Toyota Corolla parked beside her. A deader in a nurse's uniform attacked from the right. Alissa turned the wheel, pinning it against the front of the Corolla and ripping it apart. She gunned the engine, pushing aside the others. They spun around and chased after her.

At the end of the ramp, she made the turn onto the next level and into a pack of ten deaders. Alissa clipped the first one, dressed in a Boston PD uniform and missing its left arm. The deader bounced off the front fender and across the hood, rolling off to the side. Swerving to avoid the pack, she hit a young deader no more than twelve years old. Its legs shattered on impact and toppled backwards. The Subaru bounced over the body and Alissa swore she could feel its head explode under the weight of the front tires. The Forester slowed and the ride became bumpy. At first, she thought the vehicle had a flat. Checking the rearview mirror, she noticed the body of the young deader had gotten caught in the undercarriage, the rear left tire lodged against its ribcage and spinning in the gore as if on ice. Alissa applied the brakes. A dozen set of hands slapped against the windows, fingernails scratching against the surface.

Alissa ignored them. Shifting into reverse, she backed up a few yards, shifted back into drive, and shoved her foot against the accelerator. The SUV lurched forward, this time having enough traction to drive over the carcass, shattering its ribcage. Now the deaders ran along beside her, smearing the windows with bloody hands.

Making the level three U-turn, only a few deaders sauntered between the parked cars, which she easily avoided. Alissa gunned the engine, putting some distance between her and the chasing deaders. The tires squealed as she swung around onto the second level.

Half-way down, a Prius blocked her path, sitting at a forty-degree angle across from the parking space it had been pulling out of, the front pointed down the ramp, the driver's side open. The owner must have abandoned it or, judging by the puddles of blood on the cement and dripping off the handle, had been overpowered and eaten. Alissa dropped the Forester into the lowest gear possible, aimed her right front fender for the front left tire of the Prius, and accelerated. The SUV crashed into the Prius, shoving the smaller vehicle aside. Shattered glass exploded across the hood of the Forester, accompanied by the scraping of metal against metal. On the dashboard, the CHECK ENGINE and deflated tire lights burned yellow. No big deal. She would be clear of the garage soon and could check on the Subaru later.

Rounding the corner onto the final ramp, Alissa's heart sank. Two vehicles blocked her path. A Volvo had been backing out from one of the spaces along the right and was more than halfway into the ramp when someone in a black Dodge Ram pulled out, T-boning the Volvo with its back bumper. The front fenders of both vehicles were still in their parking space, making it impossible to break through. The driver's sides of both vehicles were open. Blood covered the cement, flowing beneath the Ram. A body lay between the angle of the Ram and the Volvo. She saw only one way out of this and prayed the keys were still in the Ram's ignition.

Shifting into reverse, Alissa backed up to the wall at the top of the ramp and paused. A moment later, the deaders chasing after her surrounded the Forester. As they clawed at the windows, she reached into the back seat and moved the backpack into the front seat beside her, then removed the Glock from her belt and slid the barrel under her right leg. Alissa waited, allowing all the deaders to gather around her. Shifting into drive, she accelerated down the ramp, hugging the line of vehicles parked on the left with barely a two-inch gap. Reaching the accident, she turned the steering wheel right, slamming the front of her Forester against the Volvo, blocking the deaders from getting to her.

Alissa jumped out, reached around for the backpack, and slung it over her left shoulder. Twenty to thirty deaders stood along the right flanks of the Forester, desperate to reach her. A female deader in running shorts and a tattered T-shirt crawled across the SUV's hood. Alissa stepped up, placed the barrel three inches from its face, and fired two rounds. The female deader collapsed onto the hood, blocking the other from getting across. Alissa jumped into the driver's seat of the RAM and closed the door. She leaned to one side and breathed a sigh of relief when she saw the keys were still in the ignition. Starting the pick-up, she shifted into reverse and accelerated. Nothing happened. Alissa pulled forward four feet, shifted back into REVERSE, and gunned the engine. This time the rear end of the RAM crashed into the Volvo, shoving it to the side. She kept up the pressure until the front of the Ram cleared the parking space, then backed down toward the exit, making a three-point turn in the open area by the entrance. The wooden gate sat across the ramp, not that it posed much of an obstacle. The Ram tore the gate off its mounting as it passed through into the outdoor parking lot.

Most of the deaders were either still hunting inside the hospital or had chased after the noise on the bridges spanning the Charles River. She stopped at the exit onto Blossom Street. With the parking lot clear of immediate danger, she had a moment to plan her next move.

Turning left toward Storrow Drive would be suicide. Between the gridlock, the deaders, and the police gunning down everyone in sight, she would be lucky to last ten minutes. As stupid as it sounded, her best of chance of survival would be to head back into Boston, cut through the city using back roads, and get across the Tobin Bridge before they shut down that as well. If that closed, she would be screwed in trying to get to Archer.

Turning right, Alissa headed down Blossom Street and into downtown Boston.

Chapter Eleven

I T WAS LESS than a mile to the access ramps that led to the Tobin Bridge, and from there another twelve miles to her home in Nahant. Alissa figured that, with luck, she would be home by sunset.

As Alissa rounded the corner, a line of cars stretching a block and a half from Cambridge Street obstructed her path. She stopped fifty feet from the last car in line and stood on the runner to get a better view. Traffic heading from Storrow Drive clogged Cambridge Street, preventing the cars in front of her from merging. Incredibly, a garbage truck made a three-point turn on the crowded street, banging into other vehicles and crushing two people beneath its wheels. She tried to figure a way around this mess when the realization dawned on her that the people around the truck were deaders. Dozens of them fed on the living in the vehicles near the front of the line. She had no idea if they came from the hospital or Storrow Drive. Not that it mattered. She had to get out now.

Sliding back into the Ram, Alissa shifted the pick-up into REVERSE, backed up twenty feet, and swung left onto Cardinal William O'Connell Way. In the process, she cut off a speeding Boston Police cruiser with sirens blaring and lights flashing. She half expected the officer to come after her. Instead, he blared his horn and swerved around the pick-up, colliding head on with the garbage truck that had turned around and raced back down Blossom Street. The garbage truck crushed the front end of the police cruiser and shoved the wreck out of the way.

Alissa gunned the engine and headed down Cardinal William O'Connell Way, winding her way in front of Shriner's Hospital for Children and St. Joseph's church, then turning the bend leading toward Staniford Street.

"Fuck!"

Gridlock blocked both lanes of Staniford Street, making it impossible for the five cars stopped in front of her to move. Alissa contemplated her next move.

A Ford minivan with a family of four, two vehicles in front, pulled out into the next lane to make a U-turn. Alissa jumped and screamed as an air horn blared to her left. The garbage truck had followed her and now rushed by, shaving off the Ram's sideview mirror, and T-boned the Ford, shearing it in half. The two children flew out of the rear, their seat belts torn apart by the crash, and tumbled through the air. One bounced off a nearby UPS van, leaving a blood streak against the brown paint. The other was thrown twenty feet down the road, the still moving body being crushed underneath the wheels of the garbage truck. Five deaders clung to the side of the truck, clawing at the sanitation worker holding on to the side. The crash threw them off. The sanitation worker landed head-first, its head exploding on impact. Scrambling to their feet, the deaders pounced on the body, ripping off chunks of flesh and devouring them while still warm. The truck's driver ignored the devastation, increasing speed and using his vehicle as a battering ram to clear a path on Staniford Street. He clipped the front and rear fenders of two cars in the right lane, spinning around the larger car and flipping onto its side the smaller of the two. Continuing through, he drove the front of the truck into the driver's side of a phone company van, propelling it across the sidewalk and into the façade of the building opposite where it shattered the plate-glass window. Pedestrians screamed and ran from the inevitable. The driver attempted to swerve onto Staniford Street but traveled much too fast. His truck lifted onto its right-side tires, hovered for a moment, and overturned. Its weight and speed propelled it a hundred feet along Staniford Street, ripping down a streetlamp, crushing a dozen people, and shoving four cars out of the way.

Alissa noticed none of these details. When she glanced into the side mirror and saw the garbage truck approaching, she also noticed a pack of deaders chasing it. Pulling into the opposite lane, she fell in behind the truck, keeping one hundred feet to its rear and following through the carnage. When it flipped over onto Staniford Street, she swerved to the left, taking advantage of the path it cut to maneuver around the traffic, and cut back onto the sidewalk once the larger vehicle had finally come to rest. She slowed enough to give pedestrians a chance to get out of the way.

Traffic packed Nashua Street, which led to the ramps to the Tobin Bridge. Trying to escape this way would trap her in a kill zone. With luck, she could reach the bridge from the harbor.

She continued along the sidewalk, cutting through the corner parking lot in front of West End, and bounced over the curb onto Merrimack Street. Something huge was going down a quarter of a mile away near Haymarket. The lights from a dozen police cars, firetrucks, and ambulances strobed repeatedly. No way would she get caught in that. Swinging left onto Portland Street, she rushed through the neighborhood toward Causeway Street.

Here she came upon a total clusterfuck. Traffic backed up to the Boston Gardens. Even the oncoming lanes were packed with vehicles trying to escape the outbreak. A few other cars tried using the sidewalk on her side of the street to sneak past the traffic. Two had rear ended each other a few hundred feet down, making it impossible to pass. The sidewalk on the opposite side remained open, but it was impossible to get through the lines of vehicles. She contemplated backing up and trying another road to get onto Causeway Street, but the traffic jam stretched as far as she could see. Alissa contemplated her next move. Getting out of this part of Boston by vehicle would be impossible. She thought about going into the Garden and picking up the subway from there but quickly ruled that out, knowing her chances of survival underground were slim when the outbreak reached there. That left only one option.

Grabbing the backpack and slinging it over her shoulder, Alissa abandoned the Ram and began walking.

As she approached North Washington Street, she realized what caused the gridlock. Traffic filled the street from downtown Boston all the way across the North Washington Street Bridge, blocking the vehicles trying to exit Causeway Street. Alissa felt good about her decision. She would not be able to escape the city by car. She would have to walk across the Tobin Bridge and hopefully hitch a ride once on the other side.

Screaming from behind sent a chill down her spine. Spinning around, she saw a crowd racing around the cars, deaders close behind and tackling the slower runners. The deaders outnumbered the living, and every time a human went down the rest of the pack rushed around the attack and sought out new victims. She had only minutes to make her escape. Alissa broke into a run, making her way to the sidewalk and moving as fast as possible.

When she reached the intersection of Causeway and North Washington, the situation had deteriorated rapidly. Hundreds of people left their cars behind and made their way to the bridge. The deaders behind her had approached to within a hundred feet, and another horde made its way down North Washington from the Haymarket area. In ten seconds, this area would become a slaughterhouse. She searched for a safe place to hide.

A pizza parlor sat across the street, a green neon sign in the window announcing they were open. Alissa dashed between the abandoned vehicles and pushed her way through the panicking crowd. Reaching the sidewalk, she headed for the shop. A small pack of deaders noticed her and gave chase. Alissa increased speed. Her muscles ached from the exertion and she breathed in deep, heavy gasps. After what seemed like an eternity, she reached it and entered. Spinning around, she slammed the door shut and engaged the dead bolt, and then backed away.

Alissa felt safe until she heard a bullet being chambered into a weapon.

"Get out now or I'll shoot."

Chapter Twelve

ALISSA RAISED HER hands above her head and slowly turned around. An older man with greying hair stood in the center of the parlor. She focused on the pump-action shotgun aimed at her. His hands shook and, with his finger on the trigger, Alissa worried he might accidentally shoot her. On the opposite side of the counter stood a young kid in his late teens or early twenties, dressed in a white apron, with his arm around a teenage girl who had the same facial features as the man brandishing the shotgun.

"I don't want any trouble," Alissa said.

"Then get out." The old man used the barrel of the shotgun to motion toward the exit. "Now."

"Papa, please." The teenage girl tried to stop her dad but the boy in the apron held her back. "She's not one of them."

"You don't know that." The old man shifted his gaze over his shoulder. "I'm trying to protect you."

"I promise I'm no—"

The old man shifted his attention back to Alissa. He readjusted his aim, his hands shaking worse than before.

"At least take your finger off the trigger before you kill me," Alissa pleaded.

"If you're worried about being shot then get out."

A tense moment passed before a deader in a blood-soaked policeman's uniform slammed onto the glass. Everybody inside the restaurant jumped. The old man shifted his aim toward the deader but did not pull the trigger.

"Wh-what the fuck is that?" he stammered.

"That's what you want to send me back out into. They're all over the streets."

"Papa, you can't do it. Let her stay."

Three more deaders joined the first. They covered the glass in streaks of blood as they clasped for the food inside. A young deader in a Boston sweatshirt gnawed on the pane.

The old man stepped toward the door, driving the deaders into a frenzy. "This can't be happening."

"It is, Mr. Giovani." The boy behind the counter hugged the teenage girl.

A deader in a firefighter's uniform banged its fist against the glass and snarled at the old man. He raised the shotgun. "I'll be fucked before I let you get me."

"Mr. Giovani, don't—"

Moving to the right, Alissa raced around the old man and headed for the counter as he fired a round into the face of the firefighter deader. The blast shattered the glass and propelled it back onto the sidewalk. With nothing to stop them, the other three ran into the restaurant. The old man fired, hitting one in the left shoulder and doing nothing more than blasting off its arm. Before he could reload, the other two tackled the old man to the floor and began to feed. The one-armed deader took a moment to regain its footing, staring at where its arm used to be.

When the deaders burst through, the kid had pulled the teenage girl along with him and toward the swinging doors leading into the kitchen. She resisted, crying for her father. As Alissa came around the corner of the counter, she slapped the girl across the face, placed her hands on the teenager's back, and shoved her into the kitchen. The blow snapped the teenager back out of her shock. She stared at her father one last time before heading for safety. Alissa paused, checking on the situation. The one-armed deader noticed her and rushed forward. Alissa burst into the kitchen.

"If there's another way out, head for it."

"This way." The kid took the teenage girl by her hand and headed for the rear of the kitchen.

Alissa chased after them for five feet, stopped, and spun around to face the entrance into the kitchen, her Glock raised. When the one-armed deader burst through, she fired a single round into its forehead. The bullet compacted, blowing off the top of its skull and popping the eyes from their sockets. Yet the deader did not collapse. It fell back against the sink, got its bearings, and staggered forward, its outstretched arms attempting to find the prey its eyes could not. From the other room, she heard the other two deaders snarl and head for the kitchen. Alissa turned and ran.

The teenager stood by a door leading out into a back alley. Upon seeing Alissa, she motioned to catch her attention.

"This way. Hurry."

Alissa raced through, the teenager right behind her. As Alissa raised the Glock and scanned her surroundings for danger, the kid slammed shut the metal door and pushed his weight against it. The teenager closed the hasp over the metal loop, slipped a padlock through it, and secured it as the deaders slammed into the other side. Both the kid and the teenager jumped back. Alissa instinctively raised the Glock, ready to fire. The lock held.

"Thanks." Alissa gasped, trying to catch her breath.

"You're welcome," the kid replied. "I'm John. This is Maria."

"Alissa."

"Do you know what the hell is going on?" Maria asked.

"There's some type of virus running through the city that turns people violent. And it's spreading quickly. We have to get out of here ASAP if we're going to survive." Alissa pointed north. "Where does this alley go?"

"That takes you out onto Commercial Street, right near the intersection with North Washington."

"That's where these things are massed."

"Where are you going?" John asked.

"I'm trying to get the Tobin Bridge. I live in Nahant and want to get home."

John shook his head. "Your only way to get to the bridge from here is across the North Washington Street Bridge."

"Fuck!"

Maria pointed down the alley. "We don't have to go that way. We could cut through the parking garage and approach the bridge from the river."

"That would work," John agreed.

"Do you know the way?" asked Alissa.

"Yes."

"Go. I'll provide cover."

Maria headed down the alley for several hundred feet, turned left, and cut between two apartment buildings. They emerged onto Prince Street across from the DeFelippo Playground. After checking to make certain no deaders were in sight, the trio crossed the street into the playground and made their way through the adjacent dog park, emerging onto Hull Street.

"Where now?" Alissa asked.

Maria pointed to the left and started in that direction. Alissa stopped her and lifted the Glock. "I'll lead. John, watch our rear."

They made their way along the eastern façade of the North End Garage, Alissa keeping the weapon aimed ahead of her. She heard screaming and snarling coming from the North Washington-Causeway Streets intersection two blocks away, but no humans or deaders were visible. At the end of the garage, Alissa waved for John and Maria to stop. Moving cautiously to the corner, she peered around it.

The intersection had become a charnel house. Blood smeared the gridlocked vehicles and flowed across the pavement, pouring toward the gutters and swirling into the sewers.

A pack of deaders roamed amongst the vehicles, feeding off the bodies spread across the ground. A few people had tried to escape in this direction but had not made it far. Most had been devoured to the point that, when their bodies reanimated, they could not chase their prey but crawled along the pavement. Those victims not killed in the onslaught had escaped across the North Washington Street Bridge, leading the deaders away. That was the good news.

The bad news was they needed to cross that bridge to escape the city.

Leaning back against the wall, Alissa faced the others. "There are deaders out there."

"How many?" asked Maria. John motioned for her to be quiet.

"It's hard to tell. They're mixed among the vehicles and are feeding off their victims, which means they're distracted. It looks like the rest of the deaders have already crossed the bridge. We should be able to make it out if we keep quiet and stay on our guard."

"Wait." Maria squeezed John's hand. "What about Mimi?"

"Who's Mimi?"

"Her grandmother," John answered.

"She lives with me and Papa. She's eighty-three. She won't be able to survive on her own."

Alissa did not like where this conversation was heading. "Where do you live?"

"Here in the North End."

"We can't bring her with us," said John. He focused his attention on Alissa. "Her grandmother can only walk with a cane."

Alissa frowned. "We can't take Mimi. She's too much of a liability."

"We can't leave her." Maria's voice cracked, on the verge of tears.

"It's only temporary. Once the authorities have restored

order you can come back for her."

"No." Maria shook her head several times. "She'll be scared and alone. I won't do that to her." Maria placed her hand on John's chin and turned it to her, her eyes pleading. "Come with me. Her house is only a few blocks from here. We can wait this out from there."

Alissa could tell by the pained expression on John's face that he did not want to go back into the city. For a minute, he said nothing. Maria gazed into his eyes and whispered the word, "Please?"

John wrapped an arm around Maria, pulling her close. "I'm going to stay with Maria. Can you get out of the city on your own?"

Alissa nodded. "Good luck."

"You, too." Taking Maria by the hand, John led her back down the street toward the North End.

Alissa watched them for a few seconds before turning her attention back to the matter at hand. She peered around the corner of the parking garage and, once certain no danger presented itself, rushed across the street to the school. A knocking startled her. She dropped into a crouch, her eyes trained along the Glock's site as she swung the weapon from one side to the other, searching for the threat. The knocking sounded again to her rear. It came from the first-floor windows of the school where a young woman surrounded by elementary-aged children tapped on the glass to catch her attention. The woman opened the window and yelled to Alissa.

"Can you help us?"

Alissa raised a forefinger to her lips as she approached the window. The woman ignored her.

"What's the situation like?"

"Shut up," Alissa whispered forcefully. "You want them to hear you?"

"Who?" This time the woman spoke softly. "What's going on?"

66

"There's some type of virus spreading through the city. It's highly contagious and anyone who contacts it becomes violent in seconds. Hundreds of people have been killed in the past hour."

"Dear God."

"How many of you are there?"

"A little over a hundred and thirty students, all of them elementary schoolers, and fifteen or so teachers and office staff."

"Have you called 911?"

"Several times, but we can't get through. All the land lines are jammed. We've been trying for half an hour. The staff has been attempting to reach help through their cell phones but are running into the same problem." The woman began to understand how critical the situation had become. "What should we do?"

"Do you have a room in the basement without windows?"

"We have the gym."

"Take everyone down there, then lock and bolt yourselves inside. Gather all the food and water you can because you might be there for a while."

"How long?"

Alissa could not bring herself to tell the truth. "Maybe a day or two before order is restored."

"Oh, God."

"And for Christ's sake, be quiet. Don't let the infected know you're in the basement or they'll find a way to break in. I'll let the police know you're here."

"God bless." The woman closed the window and headed off to get the children to safety.

Alissa ducked into the faculty parking lot, cutting across it diagonally to a small copes of trees that blocked the view of the school's tennis courts from the street. She made her way to a large tree close to the sidewalk and checked out the situation. Like before, only a handful of deaders were visible, and they were preoccupied with feeding. Stepping onto the sidewalk, she moved forward a few yards to get a better view of the bridge. As with the intersection, cars packed the structure, blocking all lanes leading out of the city. A handful of deaders roamed between the vehicles. God knew how many might be out of sight. The bridge stretched for a quarter of a mile and sat fifteen feet above the water so, worst case scenario, she could jump over the side and swim to shore. If she moved quickly and quietly, she should make it with no problem. Taking a deep breath, Alissa headed down the sidewalk, walking briskly and quietly.

Traversing the bridge might not be as difficult as she had imagined. A dozen or so deaders crouched between the vehicles, devouring those unlucky enough not to escape. None of them paid attention to her. She made it along the southern span and reached the swing bridge portion. Fifty feet in front of her, beneath the stairs of the control room that rested on a rusty, elevated platform, a pile of corpses sat in a pool of congealing blood. Making sure no deaders were nearby, she stepped over the metal guardrail between the sidewalk and road. She had made it halfway across with no—

Something slamming against metal startled Alissa. She aimed the Glock and scanned around her, trying to figure out the source of the noise, but saw nothing. A ferocious snarl sounded above her. A deader stood inside the control room smashed its face against the window to get at her. On the third try, it slammed against the bridge's control panel. A siren went off, a loud and tinny blare that could be heard for at least a mile. Every deader on the bridge stood up, about thirty in total, searching for the noise. Upon seeing Alissa, the pack rushed toward her from every direction.

What concerned Alissa more than the deaders was that the center span began to pivot to the left. In less than a minute, she would be trapped with no means of escape.

Chapter Thirteen

Alissa ran. Ahead of her, four abandoned vehicles sat with their front tires resting on the northern span and their rear ones on the swinging portion. The motion dragged each vehicle to the left, blocking the deaders approaching from the north, but also impeding her escape.

The bridge turned far enough that the sedan on the far left spun around and slid off into the river, taking two deaders with it. The next vehicle, a plumber's van, was parked far enough onto the northern span that it did not fall off, nor did the two cars to its right. The bridge's metal frame pushed against them until the three were shoved together side by side. They began to buckle. Alissa jumped onto the trunk of the car farthest to the right, a Lexus GS 350, and made her way to its roof. The windshields on all three vehicles shattered, showering her in shards of glass, momentarily blinding her. The car in the center, a VW Beetle, collapsed under the pressure. When the Lexus jerked left to fill the empty space, it knocked Alissa onto the hood. A second later, the rear of the van imploded. The Beetle fell against the collapsed portion and slid off the span, splashing into the river. Alissa was tossed against the side of the van, cracking her head on the side mirror. Screeching metal told her she had to move now. Scrambling to her feet, she dove off the hood and landed on her left shoulder on the trunk of the next car in line, one completely on the northern span. The backpack dug into her abdomen. The right side of the swinging span passed a few feet away, its weight crushing the van and the Lexus. Alissa did not have time to breathe a sigh of relief.

A snarling face appeared in front of her. Alissa shoved the Glock into its mouth and fired, blowing the entire back of its head off. Before the body even hit the pavement, she rolled off the trunk, ignoring the pain in her side, and ran for the right side of the bridge. The opening of the swing bridge had cut off the deaders on the southern span from reaching her, but a dozen on this side remained a threat. Alissa could not make it past them before they converged on her, and they were too close to take out all of them with gunfire. That left one option.

Reaching the sidewalk, Alissa bound over the guardrail and into the river. She sank a few feet, kicked her legs, and broke the surface. A dock floated less than a hundred feet away. She swam for it, each stroke with her left arm sending a shooting pain down her side. Behind her, three deaders fell over the guardrail. She turned, hoping these things couldn't swim. They sank to the bottom. A minute later she reached the dock, climbed up, and sat on the wooden deck, catching her breath. Part of her could not believe she had survived.

Alissa's optimism faded when she heard the thud of falling bodies.

The deaders continued along the northern span until it connected with land. One by one, they tumbled off the bridge into an adjacent parking lot. The first two crawled to their feet and charged the dock. The third snapped its leg and could not stand. Each of the other deaders landed on it, breaking limbs and creating a pile of living dead the others could not extricate themselves from. The two moving deaders approached the entrance to the dock, cutting off her only exit. Jumping up, Alissa raced down the dock and turned the L-shaped corner toward land.

Alissa paused as the first deader rushed toward her, its teeth bared and ready to feed. She raised the Glock, aimed at its forehead, and fired. The round ricocheted off its skull. She fired again. This time the bullet thudded harmlessly into its shoulder. The swaying of the dock threw off her aim. She repeatedly fired at the attacking deader. Most of the rounds missed or hit non-vital parts. The third struck it in the forehead but did not slow its charge. The sixth ripped off and its jaw and the last punched through the back of its throat, bringing it down. Forward momentum kept the body moving forward for several feet before collapsing. Alissa backed up until the first deader came to a standstill and raised the Glock to fire at the second. The slide stuck in the open position. Alissa switched out the empty magazine with a full one but did not have time to load a bullet into the chamber. The second deader had closed to within three feet and prepared to tackle her.

Alissa dropped to her hands and knees and braced. The deader tripped, kicking her in the bruised left side. The pain momentarily blurred her vision. She struggled to her feet. The deader had landed face first on the dock, shattering its front teeth and cracking its jaw. As the deader attempted to stand, Alissa shoved it, toppling it off the side. Its right hand clutched Alissa's left ankle, knocking her onto her back and dragging her toward the edge of the dock. Planting her left foot on the nearby piling, Alissa stopped herself from being dragged into the river. The deader began pulling itself up her leg, hand over hand. Any second she expected to be bitten. Alissa kicked it, slamming her right heel against its face. Once. Twice. Three times. She knocked out most of its remaining teeth and broke its lower jaw in half, the two pieces hanging loosely by the joints. The deader continued its assault. It jumped onto the dock, clutching Alissa by the upper thigh, its weight dragging her farther toward the edge. She pulled back on the Glock's slide, loading a round into the chamber.

An angry snarl came from the right. One of the deaders had broken free from the pile in the parking lot and now raced down the dock. Alissa put three rounds into the face of the deader holding her. Its grip loosened and slid into the river, disappearing beneath the surface. Rolling to her right, she clipped the legs of the charging deader, sending it sprawling. Alissa continued the roll into a crouching position, stood, and approached the deader. It tried to get up. She placed the Glock against the base of its skull and fired. A splatter pattern of blood and gore sprayed down the dock and the deader collapsed, lifeless.

Alissa checked her surroundings. Except for the pile of deaders in the parking lot, no others were in sight. Lifting the backpack onto her left shoulder and brandishing the Glock in her right hand, she set off down the dock and into the parking lot of the Residence Inn. Most of the guests and staff had already fled the city. She crossed the road into Constitution Plaza. Another parking lot sat nearby, surrounded by trees. She made her way there, found a spot where she could keep an eye on everything, and sat in the shade.

Alissa sighed. Not from an emotional outburst, but from mental and physical exhaustion. She had no idea how long she had been on the run. The past couple of hours seemed like a blur, although she knew the memories would become sharp once she got back to Nahant. If Alissa replayed all the close encounters she had gone through and all the people she had to leave behind, she would probably have a crippling anxiety attack. She couldn't afford that, especially now being so close to safety. The Tobin Bridge stood less than a mile away. In another hour, she would be out of the city and beyond the outbreak. Then she could hitch a ride home, check on Archer, and take time to plan her next course of action.

Alissa rested for ten minutes. When she stood, her muscles ached and her left side throbbed. Once she got home, she'd also have to take a hot shower and medicate the Hell out of herself.

Mounting the backpack on her shoulder, Alissa set out along Constitution Road.

Chapter Fourteen

AFTER A TEN-MINUTE walk that led her past the U.S.S. *Constitution*, Alissa emerged onto Chelsea Street. Ahead of her were the approaches to the Tobin Bridge. The top span carried the traffic from the North Shore across the bridge into the city; one hundred feet to her left, the highway went underground, passing beneath the local neighborhoods and emerging near I-93. Directly in front of her, the underground highway from the city emerged from its tunnel and connected with the lower span leading out of the city. Once on the bridge, Alissa would be across the Mystic River within a half hour and back in Nahant a few hours after that. Experiencing an optimism she had not felt since the outbreak ravaged the hospital, she crossed to the bridge.

Alissa's optimism drained away when she reached the chain-link fence imbedded into the cement guardrail along the lower span. All three lanes were jammed with cars and trucks, stretching from well into the tunnel to as far as she could see along the span. Most had been abandoned. A flow of pedestrians walked between the vehicles, not heading north out of the city but back toward the tunnel. Alissa shook the fence and called out to attract someone's attention.

"What's going on?"

An older gentleman with greying hair sticking out from under a Red Sox baseball saw her. "The shit's hitting the fan lady. What do you think's going on?"

"I mean, why aren't you heading out of the city?"

"Because the cops are being fucking assholes," answered a teenager several yards behind the older gentleman who trudged along with the others, holding his girlfriend's hand. "They won't let anyone out of the city. Keep spouting off about containing the spread of the infection, whatever that bullshit means."

Alissa did not bother clarifying. "There's hundreds of you. Why didn't you just push past them?"

"Be my guest." The teenager chuckled derisively. "There's thirty or forty Staties up there with assault rifles, clubs, tear gas, and dogs. The first ones who tried to push through were roughed up pretty bad."

"He's right," agreed the older gentleman. "We're all stuck here until the police say otherwise."

Fuck that, Alissa thought. *I'm getting out of here while I can.*

Stepping back several feet from the guardrail, she scanned the upper level. Like on the one below it, the traffic extended from deep inside the tunnel along the span as far as she could see. And, like on the lower level, everyone had abandoned their vehicles and were on foot. Except they were heading away from Boston and back toward the North Shore. A handful of State Troopers stood among them, motioning to proceed and making sure no stragglers were left behind. The police up here had enough common sense to realize that since these people had not been in Boston, they were not contagious, and were allowing them to make it to safety. She had found her way out of the city, but she had to move fast.

The retaining wall for the upper level stood ten feet in height. Fifty feet down Chelsea Street, an Xfinity installation van had been left on the side of the road. She ran over to it. Three ladders rested on racks along the right side. Alissa removed one, brought it over to the retaining wall, and placed it against the outer façade. It did not reach the top, so she extended the length and climbed. Once at the top of the ladder, it was a five-foot drop to the highway below. Alissa sat on the wall, swung her legs over the side, and pushed off. A bolt of pain shot up her left side when she landed but, other than that, there were no injuries. The others were already well ahead of her. She set off after them, rushing to catch up while trying not to attract attention.

Alissa had walked for half a mile, slowly closing the gap between her and the last stragglers. As she approached the first span over Little Mystic Channel, a State Trooper who had stayed back to help noticed her. As the last pedestrian passed by, the trooper maneuvered himself to block Alissa's path. She noticed that his right hand rested on the weapon in his holster.

"Hold up there, ma'am."

"It's okay. I may be slow, but I can make it on my own."

"Ma'am, that was not a request." The trooper gripped the weapon's handle. "I need you to stay where you are."

"Sure." Alissa stopped, her mind desperately racing to figure a way out of this. "What's wrong?"

"You need to turn around and go back into the city."

"Why?"

"Ma'am, I can't let you pass."

"I don't understand why. I haven't been in Boston."

"Really?" The trooper removed his weapon, although he did not aim it. "Then why are you covered in blood?"

Alissa mentally swore to herself. When she checked her clothes, she realized she had blood stains on her civvies from where she killed those deaders on the pier. Alissa fought to come up with a believable explanation.

"I got this trying to help someone else."

"From the city?"

"I... I don't—"

"Ma'am, you've been in contact with people from Boston, which means you may be infected. I can't let you cross this bridge."

"Please. I've not been bitten." Alissa raised her arms and turned them from side to side. "I can show you."

"Stop right there, ma'am." The trooper stepped forward. "If you try to get past me, I'm going to have use lethal force. Please back down."

Before Alissa could think of a response, the trooper mumbled and raised his weapon. She closed her eyes and waited for the gunshot. Instead, she heard snarling and the sound of running feet. Spinning around, Alissa saw deaders thronging between the abandoned vehicles. The trooper maneuvered around Alissa and fired into the pack, his bullets useless against the horde. With his magazine empty, he lowered the weapon and stared in astonishment.

"What the fuck?"

"I would run." Alissa broke into a sprint, heading north along the bridge.

The trooper followed close behind. As he ran, he reached up and pressed the TALK button on his shoulder-mounted microphone. "This is Harrelson. We have incoming. Prepare the charges."

"Say that again," came the response through the speaker.

"The infected are heading your way. You have less than a minute or we're screwed."

Alissa had driven across the Tobin Bridge hundreds of times but never realized its true length until she had to cover the distance on foot. After a few minutes, she began huffing and her heart pounded in her chest. Harrelson did not seem to be doing much better by the way he gasped and panted. By the time they reached the expanded section that used to contain the toll plaza, both had to stop and catch their breath. Alissa leaned against the cement guardrail where the booths once sat. She felt as though she would be lucky not to pass out.

The deaders had closed to within fifty yards. Harrelson swapped out the empty magazine.

"Aim for their heads," huffed Alissa. "It's your only chance of taking them down."

Harrelson fired the first two rounds into the head of the

closest deader, a woman in an expensive but gore-covered business suit and flats, blasting away everything above its jaw. The carcass tumbled to the road, blood flowing across the asphalt. Seeing that the tactic worked, the trooper double tapped the closest deaders, taking down another four before he ran out of ammunition.

Having caught her breath, Alissa began running again, with Harrelson only a few feet behind her and the deaders fifty feet beyond. Harrelson attempted to switch out magazines, discarding the empty. His fingers fumbled the new magazine, letting it drop. He stopped to pick it up, a decision that cost him his life. A deader in a city bus driver's uniform tackled Harrelson, pinning him to the cement and ravaging his neck.

Alissa waited for a deader to take her down.

Yelling caught her attention. The noise came from the northern span. Seven State troopers stood beneath the green-painted truss. Three brandished their sidearms while the other four held pump-action shotguns. The female trooper on the end called out, "Let them get closer and make every shot count."

The female trooper raised her shotgun, aiming it at Alissa.

Alissa kept running but raised her hands above her head and frantically waved. "Don't shoot. I'm not infected."

"Then get out of the fucking way."

Alissa swerved right, running along the outer barrier.

The horde closed to within thirty feet of the police line when the troopers opened fire. More than a dozen deaders dropped, were shredded by shotgun shells, or propelled backward into the other deaders. The volley caused nowhere near enough damage to stop the charge. The troopers never broke rank. Maybe they figured the onslaught would disperse them, which might have been true if those things were human. Maybe they were too stunned to think clearly. Not that it mattered, for the deaders swarmed over them like a tidal wave. The ones in front brought down six of the troopers and tore into them, the screams of the dying drowned out by the frenzy of the living dead. Only the female trooper giving the orders survived, having realized the fate that would befall her team a second before it happened. She broke into a run, a few yards behind Alissa. Being the only two living things in sight, the rest of the deaders closed in on them.

Two State troopers stood in center of the bridge, one holding a detonator and the other, a tall Latino, holding a megaphone. Alissa rapidly closed the distance despite the burning in her chest and lungs. The Latino trooper started yelling, "Haul ass! Haul ass! Haul ass!"

Alissa harnessed every ounce of strength and surged forward. When she reached the Latino trooper, he stepped in front of her and blocked her path. Unable to stop, she tried to swerve around him, but he sidestepped her and reached out for her arm, nearly yanking it out of its socket.

"Where do you think you're going?"

"I'm trying to get off the bridge."

"I can't allow that." The Latino trooper withdrew his sidearm from its holster. "You're infected."

"It's okay," panted the female trooper as she approached. "She's with—"

Two muffled explosions went off on the bridge a hundred feet to the south. They had intended to destroy the southern supports to one span of the upper level, dropping that end onto the lower level, creating a roadblock below and a gap above that would prevent anyone getting into or out of Boston. This would also make it easier to repair the bridge once the outbreak had been brought under control. However, intent does not always translate into practice. Whether through fear or being rushed, the engineers who had planted the explosives used too much, in the process weakening the supports that suspended the lower level. When the southern end up the upper span dropped onto the one below, the combination of the weakened structure and the weight of the upper span caused the lower one to collapse as well. Both spans, each one hundred feet in length, broke free and plummeted into the Mystic River, bouncing off the concrete support column before splashing into the water. The deaders continued their frenzied dash, flowing off the southern span like a waterfall of dead flesh, freefalling into the river. Alissa heard the splashing of the bodies as they slammed into the water.

Alissa started walking north. She made it only a few feet when the Latino trooper raised his firearm again. "Stop or I'll be forced to shoot."

"Cut the shit, Rodriguez." The female trooper approached him. "You can see she's not one of them."

Rodriguez spun the firearm and aimed it at the female trooper. "How do I know you're not infected?"

The female trooper stiffened and her demeanor went from annoyed to furious. "You put that fucking gun away or I will—"

The span they stood on, adjacent to the one that had collapsed, vibrated, followed by the cracking of cement and the straining of steel. Alissa dashed for safety. Rodriguez chased after her. The southern end of the span dropped, slamming into the deck below. The female trooper cried out as she rolled down the length of the collapsed span and plummeted into the river, joining the flow of deaders still racing lemming-like to their doom. Alissa had crossed over to the next span. Rodriguez had not and, when it collapsed, he fell. He had forethought enough to reach out and grab the northern end, preventing himself from sliding to his death. Alissa rushed over to the edge and fell prone, staring over the side at the river two hundred and fifty feet below. She extended her arm.

"Take my hand. I'll help you up."

"Don't let me die."

"I'll try."

The other two troopers came up beside her. One dropped prone and reached over the edge to help his friend as the second lifted Alissa off the cement and gently nudged her away, joining the other trooper in trying to save their friend. Alissa had withdrawn thirty feet when a sharp, metallic groan cut through the silence. A moment later, the second section collapsed, taking the three State Troopers with it. It pancaked onto the span along the lower level and dislodged it. Both plunged into the river.

Alissa responded with the only logical course of action available. She spun around and ran north as fast as possible before the rest of the bridge came apart. It suffered no further structural collapse, not that it mattered to Alissa, who did not stop until she had reached the on ramp from Chelsea to the upper span. Slipping off her backpack and placing it on the ground, she leaned against the cement guardrail and slid into a seating position. Leaning her head back against the cement, she closed her eyes and concentrated on catching her breath, which took several minutes.

Her gaze focused on the portion of the bridge that had collapsed. Slowly it dawned on Alissa. She was the last one out of Boston, at least via this route. After what she witnessed, she hoped none of the deaders made it out otherwise no one would be able to put an end to this. Her mind wandered to the thousands of people trapped inside and the....

No! she chastised herself. *Don't dwell on them. You're not safe yet.*

Alissa still had to make her way home, a trip of about twelve miles. The worst part, she had no idea what the situation was outside of Boston. For all she knew, the deaders could have escaped the city from other directions and were spreading across the state. Normally she would consider herself paranoid for thinking that way but, after today, she would rather be overly cautious than dead. With luck, she might be able to hitch a ride part of the way home. In any case, she would never make it back to Nahant unless she got her ass in gear.

Alissa stood. The pain on her left side caused her to wince. At least it didn't affect her breathing, which indicated no internal damage. For the first time in hours she also noticed the throbbing in her right hand where the pinky had been dislocated. Unfortunately, she had lost the bag with the medicines, bandages, and blood samples; she sure could use those pain killers now. And she really needed a jacket. Her clothes were soaked with sweat from all the running and, now that the sun had begun to set, the weather grew colder. She would be freezing by the time she made it home, although a bad cold would be a small price to pay for being alive.

It suddenly dawned on Alissa that she stood by the on ramp from Chelsea. She peered around the guardrail, crouching and being careful not to be spotted. Three police cruisers sat at the entrance, blocking the path. The six officers wore riot gear and carried pump-action shotguns. On the other side of the street sat an Army National Guard two-and-a-half-ton truck. Civilians filled half the back deck while two guardsmen stood ten feet away, each brandishing an automatic weapon. Though hard to determine from this distance, none of those detained seemed like looters. They ranged in ages from young kids to the elderly. A few of them she recognized by their clothing when they were ahead of her on the bridge before the deader attack. The police examined everyone for wounds. When a person passed inspection, they were allowed through the checkpoint and ushered over to the truck where troops helped them on board. Alissa assumed they were under detention after escaping from the city and would most likely be taken to a center until the crisis blew over. She remembered the news reports from New Orleans after Katrina and had worked with a nurse who went down there with FEMA to assist those who had survived the hurricane. The stories she brought back were horrifying. No fucking way would she let herself be taken to one of those hell holes.

As Alissa watched, one of the younger cops checking out a man in his early to mid-thirties suddenly stepped away and reached for his sidearm.

"Jesus Christ, he's infected." The officer's excited tone spooked the others, especially the civilians, worsening the situation.

"I'm fine." The man raised his hands. Palms open, to chest level.

"You've been bit." The scared officer raised his weapon and aimed it at the man's chest.

A woman and young girl about eight years old were next in line, presumably his family. The girl cried and hugged her mother, burying her face against her mother's waist. The woman pleaded, "Please don't shoot him."

An older police officer with greying hair stepped up beside the younger one, positioning himself in front of the latter but not in the line of fire. "Calm down, Bill. What's going on?"

"He's been bit." The young officer pointed with his weapon. "He's going to turn."

The older officer faced the man. He kept his manner calm and reassuring. "Is that true, sir?"

"Yes, but it didn't break the skin." The man pulled his collar aside, revealing teeth marks. "See. It's not even bleeding."

By now everyone else bordered on panic. The police and military had their weapons drawn and ready, most aimed at the man, several drawing down on the other civilians waiting at the checkpoint or in the back of the truck. The older officer attempted to diffuse the situation.

"Everybody, calm down." He stepped over to the infected man. "Can I see the wound, please?"

"I f-feel fine."

"I understand, but I still need to assess it."

The man looked over to his wife. She nodded. He leaned forward, allowing the older officer to examine it. Indentations from the teeth were noticeable but most had not punctured skin. However, the two incisors had broken through, small trickles of blood oozing from the wounds.

The young officer aimed his weapon. "See. I told you he's infected."

"Holster that weapon now or I'll relieve you of your duties."

As the young officer unwillingly obeyed, the older officer directed his attention back to the man. "How did you get that?"

"One of those... rioters... things... attacked my family while we were trying to get out of the city."

"Were any of your family bitten?"

The man shook his head. "What are you going to do to me?"

"I have to isolate you."

"No!" yelled his wife.

The officer held up his hand, warning her to be quiet, and kept his eyes on the man. "It's merely a safety precaution. If you are infected, we can't risk having you infect others."

"What about my family?"

"You'll all go the same center, you'll just be kept in confinement until we're certain you're safe. Your family can check on you whenever they want. Is that acceptable?"

The man relaxed a bit. "It is."

"Good. I'm going to take you to the squad car to keep you isolated. Okay?"

The man went with the officer.

"Daddy!"

The little girl broke free from her mother and rushed toward her father. He went for his daughter, trying to tell her everything would be okay. The sudden movement panicked the younger officer who fired three rounds, all of which struck the man in the chest. His daughter stopped and shrieked at the sight of her father dead on the ground. Most of the civilians screamed, terrified that they would be next, a fear not alleviated by the police and military training their weapons on them.

"God damn it," yelled the older officer. "Everybody, stand

down. John, take Bill's weapon away from him."

Alissa ducked behind the retaining wall, stifling her own fears that threatened to overwhelm her. She could understand things falling apart in Boston where the outbreak occurred, but not out this far. During her career she had met enough police and military personnel to know that these people did not panic easily. That meant the situation had to be much worse than even she imagined. That also meant that no one was safe anywhere near the city. She needed to get home as quickly as possible.

Chapter Fifteen

ALISSA WALKED FOR less than a mile, still on the elevated highway, when she came upon two vehicles pulled off to the side in the breakdown lane—a Hertz van which had rear ended a VW Pissat. The accident did not seem bad enough for anyone to be hurt. They most likely were abandoned when the evacuation occurred. Making her way over to the Pissat, she checked the front and back seats. Nothing but a baby's car seat and a stuffed zebra in back, some McDonald's wrappers and bags in front, and a bottle of water in the cupholder. Finding the driver's side unlocked, she pulled it open, popped the trunk, and closed the door. Various items packed the trunk. Rummaging through it, Alissa found nothing of use. A case of Cherry Coke. A few used paperback novels, mostly trashy romances. Containers of oil, anti-freeze, and windshield wash. Yes! She found a sweatshirt with a hood buried at the bottom. She yanked it out. It bore the alligator head and blue and orange logo for the Florida Gators. Even more important, the sweatshirt fit. Now she wouldn't freeze on the walk home.

As Alissa slid it over her head and pulled it down around her waist, lights approached from the north. A State Police squad car cruised the highway, its high beams on and its blue lights flashing. Maybe she could arrange a ride home. Then she spotted a second set of headlights behind the squad car belonging to an Army National Guard two-and-a-half-ton truck. Shit. Rather than helping those who escaped, the bastards were rounding them up.

Closing the trunk, Alissa took the backpack and circled around to the right of the Pissat, lying face down between the car and the guardrail. She contemplated pulling the Glock from her waistband in case she needed it but decided otherwise. She would never be able to outgun two Staties and God knows how many guardsmen. Instead, she lay low and prayed they would not find her.

The squad car pulled to a stop adjacent to the Pissat.

"Is anyone there?"

A few seconds of silence.

"I said, is anyone there?"

A different, accented voice said, "I told ya there was nothing."

"I saw the light go on in the car."

"Ya saw a reflection. Come on. Let's finish this run and get back to the station."

The passenger door to the squad car opened. From her view underneath the Pissat, she saw two feet step onto the cement.

"Where are ya going?"

"I want to make sure no one's hiding in the car."

"For Christ's sake, will ya get back in—"

"*All available units. Proceed immediately to I-93 North in Somerville.*"

"What's going on?" asked the accented voice.

"*The infected broke through our barricades and are attacking Sullivan Square. The units there are about to be overrun.*"

"On our way." Then, to the trooper standing outside the squad car, "Ya heard the lady. Come on."

The trooper climbed back in as the driver switched on the lights and siren. Both vehicles sped away, heading south toward Somerville. Alissa waited until she could no longer see their taillights before getting up. She needed to get back home before the entire metro area fell apart.

Alissa's first chance to get off the highway undetected came when the elevated portion merged with the ground near Chelsea High School. She climbed over the guardrail, made her way down the embankment, and continued to the intersection where she stopped to get her bearings. She stood on Source Street. That name sounded familiar. It took a few seconds but she remembered. Waze had taken her this way once when the police closed the Revere Beach Parkway due a traffic jam. If she turned right one block onto Everett Avenue and followed that a few blocks to Broadway, she could take that road right into Revere. From there, it was only a short jaunt home.

She walked for five miles through residential neighborhoods, shocked at how little activity she saw. Only a handful of people were out and about despite the early evening hour. She came across three families hurriedly packing their belongings and pets into their vehicles, obviously preparing to evacuate. Most of the homes she passed had lights on; through the living room windows she noticed TVs tuned to the local or cable news, which did not surprise her. Whenever a disaster or tragedy occurred, more people tuned in to find out the details, especially when so close to home. She wondered if the media reported all the facts, or if they were even being told what was really happening.

Alissa found a similar situation when she reached the Revere Beach Parkway. A dozen vehicles traveled the road, usually one of the busiest in the area. Businesses remained open, although few cars filled the parking lots. Only a handful of people were at the local restaurants and Planet Fitness. It felt more like midnight than dinner time. Only Home Depot had a packed lot and a booming business.

When she finally reached Revere Beach, Alissa felt the first sense of relief she had all day. A few miles across the sound sat Nahant, the island where she lived. From this distance it appeared normal. Lights shone in windows and the island seemed peaceful. A far cry from what she had experienced. It presented a sharp contrast to the beach itself. Normally vibrant and filled with pedestrians, even in winter, tonight not a soul strolled the sidewalk and not a single car parked or cruised the road. She sat on the seawall and pulled the hood over her head to deflect the cold blowing in from the ocean. Removing one of the bottles of water from her backpack, she unscrewed the top and took a long swig, then listened to the soothing sound of the waves lapping against the shore.

A ping sounded from the backpack. It came from her cell phone. Unzipping the outer pocket, Alissa pulled it out and checked. Paul had sent her a text more than three hours ago. Punching in her four-digit code, she opened the phone and read the message.

STUCK IN PITTSBURGH. SHIT HIT THE FAN HERE. AM HEADING FOR THE CABIN. I ADVISE YOU DO THE SAME. SITUATION OUT OF CONTROL. MAY BE ONLY SAFE SPOT. IF YOU GET THERE BEFORE ME, PASS-WORD IS YOUR BIRTHDAY IN EIGHT NUMBERS. GOOD LUCK AND TRUST NO ONE.

Shit, things must really be bad if Paul was telling her to meet him at the cabin. She had planned on heading there anyways. She only needed a way to get there.

Billy! With everything going down, she had almost forgotten about her brother stationed in Iraq with an engineering battalion. Alissa called up his number from her contact list and pressed CALL. No connection. She tried four more times. On the last attempt, a recorded female voice announced that all circuits were busy and urged she try again later. Instead, Alissa typed a text message.

I'M SAFE. MADE IT OUT OF BOSTON AND AM ON MY WAY HOME TO NAHANT. HOW ARE YOU DOING?

Alissa hit SEND. She slid the phone in her jacket pocket when it pinged. Pulling it out, she punched in her passcode, excited to hear from her brother. A redline enclosed her text message with a notification underneath stating MESSAGE COULD NOT BE DELIVERED.

Shit.

Pushing off the seawall, Alissa continued down the beach. She had walked for ten minutes when she heard an engine approaching from behind. A red Nissan Pathfinder cruised along the beach road. She focused on the occupants, an older man and woman who seemed safe enough. Stepping over to the curb, she waved her hands, hoping the couple would stop. She smiled as the Pathfinder slowed and the passenger's window rolled down.

"Are you all right?" asked the woman.

"Yes. I was hoping I could hitch a ride with you."

The driver leaned over. "Where are you going?"

"Nahant."

"We can take you as far as the road leading out to Nahant. Is that okay?"

"That's perfect." Alissa opened the rear door, tossed her backpack inside, and slid into the seat.

"I appreciate the ride. I'm Alissa."

The woman shifted in her seat. "I'm Darlene. This is my husband Tom."

Tom waved while keeping his eyes on the road. "You're lucky we found you."

"Why?"

"Martial law has been declared. A curfew has been put into place for the entire metropolitan area from sunset to sunrise. The police have been threatening to arrest anyone out after dark and send them to a detention center."

That explained why so few people were around. "I've seen a lot of people breaking curfew."

"The police are overwhelmed," responded Tom. "They're only arresting those causing trouble or anyone that came out of Boston."

"The Revere Police stopped us a few miles back," said Darlene. "They didn't hassle us once they found out where we're going."

"Where's that?"

"To stay with our daughter and grandson in Gloucester. We'd rather be with them... just in case."

"I understand."

"We figured we go now," added Tom. "By this time tomorrow, the state will be completely locked down. By the weekend, all of New England."

Alissa's mind went back to the incident at the Chelsea on ramp. An awkward silence passed before she asked, "How bad is it?"

Tom shook his head in frustration. "We stopped watching the news after the governor declared martial law and imposed the curfew."

"It's bad," added Darlene. "The police and National Guard stopped the infected—"

"They're looters and rioters," Tom spat.

"—from crossing over into Cambridge and the North Shore but weren't as fortunate to the south. They've spread as far as Brookline, Roxbury, and South Boston."

"Jesus," Alissa mumbled under her breath.

"That isn't the half of it." Tom reached the end of Revere Beach and veered off onto North Shore Road, crossing the small bridge that led into Lynn. Traffic here was as light as everywhere else. "The local news reported that riots were breaking out in other cities across the country. Damn social unrest is spreading. That's why we're heading to our daughter's." Tom took his right hand off the steering wheel long enough to reach into his jacket pocket and withdraw a .38 revolver so Alissa could see it.

They drove in silence along the Lynnway for the next ten minutes until they reached a rotary. Tom pulled over to the side and parked in front of a long road heading south. "This is as far as we go."

"That's okay." Alissa opened the car door. "Thank you so much for the ride."

"Our pleasure."

Darlene reached her right hand into the back seat. "Good luck and God bless."

Alissa shook Darlene's hand. "I'll need it."

"Sadly, we all will."

Alissa climbed out. Tom pulled away as Darlene waved. Alissa watched the car as it headed down Lynn Shore Drive and then turned around. The four-lane causeway ahead of her ran for a mile, paralleling the man-made beach connecting the shore with the island. She set off, looking forward to being home soon.

The walk gave her time to think. Rather than rehash everything that had happened in the last twelve hours, she focused on the serenity of her surroundings, an overpowering serenity. The waves lapped against the rocky foundation of the causeway, a sound she always found soothing. Few other noises interrupted the rhythmic tide. No cars traveled the causeway, which was unusual. Across the cove, the only sounds came from a woman's scream, a gunshot in the distance, and a police car with sirens blaring racing along Revere Beach, its flashing blue lights eerily reflected off the water. The quiet had a calming effect, lulling her into a sense of security.

All that changed as Alissa approached the shores of Little Nahant. Several bright lights flashed on, illuminating her. She closed her eyes. A voice called out in a threatening tone, "Turn around and go back where you came from. No one is allowed in."

"But I live here."

"Nice try."

"It's true."

The sound of weapons being readied came from behind the lights. "This is your last warning."

"I live at 136 Willow Road."

A pause. "Okay. Approach slowly with your hands above your head. And don't try anything foolish."

The floodlights went out. Alissa raised her hands and approached. As her vision adjusted to the dark, she noticed seven cars at the entrance to the island. Four blocked the roads on and off; the others were parked behind them, their front ends arranged to cover the gaps between the blocking vehicles to ensure nothing could bust through. When one hundred feet from the cars, she stepped over a string of spike strips laid across the road to blow out the tires of anyone trying to run the barricade. Three men dressed in civilian clothes came around from behind the cars. Two stepped to either side of the gap, holding semi-automatic weapons. The other stood between the front and rear fenders and used his hand to motion her forward. He made a show of keeping his right hand on the handle of his holstered sidearm.

"Let me see your license."

"It's in my backpack."

He patted the hood. "Get it out. Slowly."

Alissa slowly unzipped it. He motioned for her to stop and pulled the rear of the pack down, shining a flashlight inside before allowing her to proceed. Alissa reached in and rummaged around for her wallet. After a few seconds the realization dawned on her—she usually kept her wallet in the glove compartment of the Forester, which she left behind in the hospital parking garage. When she made eye contact with him, the panic on her face must have been evident.

"I'm sick of this bullshit." He stepped back behind the blockade, pointing to his two companions. "Send the bitch on her way."

One of them picked up Alissa's backpack and shoved it into her chest. The second grabbed her by the forearm and yanked her away from the cars, pushing her toward the causeway. Fear welled up inside her.

She had never been as happy to see flashing blue lights and the buzz of a police siren as at that moment. A Nahant Police squad car pulled up to the barricade and stopped. Two officers climbed out. As the younger of the two stood in the background, the other approached the blockade.

"What's going on here, Johnny?"

The guy who had ordered her sent away became more subdued. "I'm doing what the chief asked us to. I'm making sure no one gets onto the island who doesn't belong here."

"The chief asked you to set up a roadblock, not form a God damn posse." He moved between the two vehicles, forcing Johnny to back away. The two with the semi-automatic weapons lowered the barrels and stepped back several paces. The officer raised his flashlight, not into her face like an interrogation but enough to see her features. His eyes widened.

"Alissa?"

Alissa shaded the light from her eyes. "Nathan, is that you?"

"I thought you were trapped in Boston."

"I barely made it out alive. I was on my way home when I ran into these...." Alissa's gaze shifted between the three harassers.

"Jesus." Nathan spun around and shined the light directly into Johnny's face. "What the fuck are you doing?"

"S-she had no proof she lived here. The chief told us to make sure only residents made it back to the island."

"You don't have to be an asshole about it." Nathan turned back to Alissa. "Are you all right?"

"Yes."

"Did any one rough you up?"

Alissa stared at the two men with the semi-automatic weapons. They averted their gaze.

Nathan took Alissa's backpack and swung it over his shoulder, then gestured for her to pass through the blockade. The other civilians gave them a wide berth. As Nathan passed by

Johnny, he said, "You and I are having a long talk later."

"Yes, sir."

When they reached the squad car, Nathan tossed the backpack into the rear seat and opened the front door for Alissa. She climbed in and he circled around to the driver's side. Before getting in, he motioned to the other officer.

"Mark, stay here with this bunch and make sure they don't get into any more trouble. I'll be back in half an hour."

"Roger that."

Nathan turned the car around and headed along Nahant Road. He did not talk on the drive to her house, which Alissa appreciated. She and Nathan had known each since they attended Nahant High School back when he was a jock and she was one of the brainy kids. Her friends told Alissa that Nathan had a crush on her but didn't have enough courage to ask her out. They graduated and Nathan joined the police force while she attended an out-of-state college. She came back four years later with a nursing degree and a husband, the latter disappointing Nathan more than he let on. They remained good friends, often meeting for lunch or coffee, comparing war stories as first responders. When she and Paul separated last year, Alissa thought Nathan would ask her out. In fact, she had hoped he would. He didn't and she never worked up the courage to ask him, each afraid of ruining the friendship.

Nathan pulled up in front of her residence, a two-story house on Willow Road overlooking Dorothy Cove with a view of Revere and, in the distance, the Boston skyline. He kept the engine running.

"Are you okay?"

"I am now." Alissa squeezed his hand in a friendly manner. "Thankfully, you were there to help me."

"I can't even begin to comprehend what you've gone through. All the local police are reporting it's much worse than the news is telling us."

"Trust me, it's bad out there."

"We can compare notes tomorrow." An awkward pause. "Do you wa… need me to come in with you?"

"I'll be fine. But could you wait until I get inside before leaving?"

"Of course."

Alissa got out and walked up the driveway. Her house keys were still on the keychain left in the Forester. Paul always left his keys at home, so they installed an electronic lock for the garage. She punched in the security code and pressed ENTER. The garage door raised. She gave Nathan a thumbs-up.

"Thanks again."

"No problem. Can I check in on you in the morning?"

Alissa smiled. "I'd like that."

Nathan waved and drove away. Alissa watched until the taillights of his car turned the corner before entering the garage, lowering the door behind her.

Chapter Sixteen

A LISSA ENTERED HER house through the garage entrance, stepping into the laundry room and placing the backpack on the washing machine.

"Archer, I'm home."

No response.

"Archer?"

A crash of breaking glass echoed from the kitchen. Alissa tensed. A few seconds later, the patter of tiny feet approached the laundry room and Archer stuck his head around the jamb. His tail swished even though his yellow eyes had a dissatisfied glare about them. He meowed loudly, protesting that she had missed his feeding time.

"I missed you, too, asshat."

Archer ran over and rubbed himself against her legs. Alissa picked up the cat and cuddled him. He leaned his head against her chest and purred. They hugged each other for close to a minute before Archer grew restless. She put him on the floor, patted his back, and headed for the kitchen. Archer followed, meowing the whole time.

Alissa found three glasses smashed on the floor by the island.

"Cat, you're asking for a beating."

Archer stared at her and meowed.

Alissa went to the cupboard, withdrew a bowl and a can of cat food, and prepared Archer's dinner on the counter. He jumped up and raced over, practically pushing her hands out of the way so he could eat. While he fed, she retrieved the broom and dustpan from the closet and swept up the shards. Only after she had cleaned the floor and refilled Archer's water bowl did she take off the Gators hoodie and pull a plastic bottle of cold water from the refrigerator, drinking most of it in one long gulp. When finished, she pulled out a second bottle. She would tend to her wounds and take a much-needed shower in a few minutes. First, she needed a drink. Maneuvering around the island to the counter where she stored the alcohol, she thumbed through the bottles, mostly red and white wines. None of these were strong enough to dull the adrenaline rush flowing through her. Stepping over to the refrigerator, Alissa withdrew a bottle of Stolichnaya, removed a water glass from the cabinet, and headed for the living room, leaving Archer to his meal.

Dropping onto the sofa, Alissa kicked off her shoes, poured half a glass of vodka, and took a long drink. It burned going down, not that she minded. It made her feel alive. She refrained from turning on the television, needing to distance herself from reality. Swinging her feet onto the sofa, she reclined onto the cushions. Archer jumped up beside her, climbed into her lap, and settled in for a nap. She could use one as well. Maybe after a few more swigs.

Alissa's mind began to wander. A nurse friend's husband, a veteran of Afghanistan, had told her once that in combat you only had time to react and your mind stored the events so you could recall them later. Now she understood what he meant. As the alcohol relaxed her, Alissa's mind replayed in detail the events of the day, from the outbreak in the ER until she arrived at the roadblock. It flooded her thinking, seeming unreal even though she experienced every moment. What her thoughts dwelled on most, and constantly returned to, were those people she had left behind. Courtney and Stella on the roof of the hospital, whom she gave one Glock and two bullets to. Jim Brody, who she euthanized, and the other patients on the fourth floor she left to be eaten. Doctor Edwards who asked her to take the blood samples and whom she did nothing to save. Marjorie and the others in Labor and Delivery who died because of her incompetence. John and Maria from the pizzeria, who she allowed to go back into the city to rescue her grandmother. The students and teachers she left behind at the school, lying to them about help being on its way. The police officer on the Tobin Bridge. People she should have helped. People she all but killed. Every time they crossed her memory, Alissa took a drink of vodka, hoping to drown out their image. It did little good. Guilt wracked her. She had taken an oath to do no harm. Instead, she allowed all those people to die so she could escape, so she could make it home safely. Those faces would haunt her for the rest of her life.

Alissa lifted the glass to her lips only to find it empty. She could have leaned forward to refill it, but that would have disturbed Archer. Instead, she laid back on the cushions, closed her eyes, and fell asleep.

Chapter Seventeen

S UNLIGHT STREAMED THROUGH the window and landed on Alissa's face, making it difficult to sleep. Of course, that did not bother her as much as Archer standing on her chest, his nose two inches from hers, meowing incessantly. She tried to ignore him despite the fact the noise sounded like a freight train, aggravating the headache she already had from her hangover. When she refused to open her eyes, Archer began tapping her nose with his paw. Giving in to the inevitable, Alissa opened her eyes, squinting at the light. Archer stopped harassing her. He walked farther up her chest, lowered his head, and rubbed his forehead across hers. Alissa reached up with her right hand and petted him. The cat closed his eyes and purred.

"You're an asshat, but I love you."

Archer meowed, almost as if he understood her, and jumped onto the floor.

Alissa tried to stand, not knowing what bothered her more, the pounding headache, the dry mouth, or the dullness that weighted down her stomach. She picked up the empty water glass, only then realizing how much she had drunk and feeling lucky she only felt this miserable.

Her first attempt to get off the sofa did not go well, her stomach, head, and muscles protesting the sudden movement. She fell back onto the cushions, causing Archer to dive off and bolt into the kitchen. Alissa gave her senses several seconds to settle down and tried again, this time much slower. Everything still ached or churned, but she made it to a standing position and staggered across the living room, trying to get her footing. As she entered the kitchen, Archer ran over to his empty food bowl and began another chorus of high-pitched meowing.

"Shut up, cat," Alissa teased.

Alissa crossed over to the sink, filled the glass with cool water, and drank. The liquid moistened her parched mouth and throat. Unfortunately, it did not settle as well with her stomach. After the first few gulps, she felt the bile rising and spent the next two minutes heaving into the sink. Once Alissa hacked up the last chunks of vomitus, she turned on the faucet and flushed the mess down the drain, and then refilled the glass. This time she drank slowly, spitting out the first few mouthfuls to clean her mouth.

Archer stared up at her, his head tilted at an angle.

"I'll be all right."

Archer walked over to her, slapped her leg a few times, and meowed.

"You're all heart, cat."

Alissa took a plastic container of catnip treats from the cabinet and poured half a cup into his bowl. Archer shoved her hand out of the way to get to the food. Alissa placed the container back in the cabinet and took the glass of water upstairs. Five minutes later, she had stripped out of her bloodied clothes and stood beneath a steaming hot shower. She took extra care cleaning herself, making certain she washed away all the blood and gore, then stood under the pulsating stream for several minutes. It had the desired effect. The throbbing in her head subsided, though that could have been the three Aleve she popped before turning on the water. The aches in her muscles lessened, with the downside being she became more aware of the intense pain in her side and the pinky on her right hand. When she finally shut off the water and stepped out of the shower, she tamped herself down with a towel.

The bathroom drawers and medicine cabinet had every-thing Alissa needed to tend to her wounds. Her pinky had full mobility, but it hurt like a son of a bitch when she moved it. Using bandages and an emery board she broke in half, she created a makeshift splint for the finger. The ribs were not as easy to care for. Alissa checked herself in the mirror. A heavy bruise formed beneath the ribcage under her left arm, a black and blue seven or eight inches long and three or four inches wide. The area was extremely tender, causing her to wince when she pressed against it, but not the excruciating pain she would have expected with a broken rib, nor did she suffer from chest pains or trouble breathing. The bruise should heal in a few weeks. Until then, it would be uncomfortable.

Slipping on her comfort clothes—a three-year-old pair of sweatpants and an oversized t-shirt with the faded logo of Mount Washington on the front—Alissa pocketed a roll of bandages and headed downstairs to the kitchen. Pulling open the freezer, she scooped a handful of ice into a drinking glass then rummaged around the contents until she found a frozen bag of peas. She filled the glass with water and took everything into the living room, placing it on the coffee table and switch-ing on the remote. The television had been tuned to the Hallmark Channel but, instead of showing some sappy romance, it played a newsfeed from CNN about the crisis. Alissa did not listen, instead preoccupied with placing the bag of peas on her bruised ribs and securing it with one of the bandages, which took forever when trying that maneuver alone. At first, the bag chilled her, but after a minute the cool felt good on her throbbing skin. Leaning back, she concentrat-ed on the news.

The situation had deteriorated rapidly since yesterday. Outbreaks had occurred in most major cities in America and, according to unconfirmed reports, in hundreds of small towns and cities across the country. The major anchors switched from the newsroom to on-the-scene reports from various locations.

Every segment showed death and chaos but, since most of the reporters were kept at a safe distance from the center of the action, nothing on the screen compared to being in the middle of the nightmare. The closest accurate representation occurred in Los Angeles where a busty blonde and her cameraman were overrun on live TV by the deaders. Three of the things tackled the blonde and tore her apart before the connection was severed and switched back to the stunned anchors in the newsroom. Alissa switched from channel to channel. Each station broadcast pretty much the same reports. MSNBC ran cell phone camera footage downloaded to the Internet taken by someone making the obligatory *Hajj* to Mecca in Saudi Arabia; the outbreak had occurred inside the Great Mosque near the Kaaba and, within minutes, thousands of pilgrims had turned and were feeding off those nearby. Similar footage came out of Rio de Janeiro, Paris, Moscow, Tokyo, and Beijing, although the video from Beijing also showed government troops gunning down living and living dead alike.

Alissa switched over to BBC America. Almost every country with an open press reported similar outbreaks in major cities and towns, with the symptoms being identical. Even those countries like Iran and North Korea that maintained tight control over their media could not prevent rumors of the outbreak from reaching the west through the Internet and cell phones. Like their American counterparts, none of the European or Asian pundits could identify what caused this pandemic.

Changing to local news stations offered no hope. In fact, Alissa found it more frightening because it hit so close to home. The Boston stations described in detail the spread of the virus. The closing of the bridges over the Charles River and the disabling of the Tobin Bridge had stopped the advances into Cambridge and the North Shore, although only temporarily. Routes 90 and 93 served as a conduit for the virus, much like arteries in the human bodies. First responders in the metropolitan area had been overwhelmed and even the National Guard could not stem its advance. The outbreak had spread as far north as Melrose, Stoneham, and Woburn, as far west as Waltham and Newton, and as far south as Dedham, Milton, and Braintree. Similar occurrences were reported in Portsmouth, Concord, and Manchester in New Hampshire, although the outbreaks in the first two cities had been contained so far.

Switching through the channels, she came upon the beginning of a live news conference on FOX News' affiliate in Atlanta, Georgia with Dr. SanGiovanni of the Center for Disease Control. The doctor announced the others who stood behind the podium with her and then read her prepared statement. Alissa turned up the volume.

"Please save your questions until I've given you all the facts that we currently have. Unfortunately, we don't know much. As you all are aware, an unidentified virus has broken out in every major city and thousands of small cities and towns across the United States. We've been unable to identify the virus, or where it came from. All we know is that the virus is highly contagious and turns violent those who are infected. The CDC has been in contact with the White House and most of the country's governors. For those locations not already under martial law, we strongly recommend that everybody stay indoors. If you're home, stay inside, close your windows, lock your doors, and do not let anyone in. If you are at work or school, shelter in place and wait until this virus either burns itself out or the authorities can get to you and transport you to a safe location. I know a lot of people are going to try and make it home to be with their loved ones and we can't stop that. If you do, consider that the more people who are around you the faster this virus spreads, so if you do travel you are taking your lives into your own hands. Are there any questions?"

Every reporter in the auditorium raised their hands. San-Giovanni chose an African-American gentleman seated in the front row.

"Irv Tucker with WXIA News. You suggested a moment ago for people to close their windows. Does this mean the virus is airborne?"

"No," SanGiovanni responded. "Every report that we've received so far indicates the only means of spreading the virus is through the transmission of bodily fluids, in most cases by the infected biting the intended victim. However, it's too early to determine if this is the only way to spread the infection, so we're urging keeping windows closed as a precautionary measure until we know more about it."

"When will that be?"

"I honestly can't say. However, the CDC is working closely with the World Health Organization and other scientists across the globe to isolate the virus and find a way to stop it. Next question."

Again, dozens of hands went up. SanGiovanni pointed to a redhead in the third row.

"Melissa Murphy, BBC. I have a two-part question if you don't mind."

"Go ahead."

"You said the infection is spread by the exchange of bodily fluids, mostly through the infected biting the victims. Could any type of fluid exchange result in infection, such as getting their blood on you?"

Alissa's eyes popped open. She had been covered in deader blood all day.

"It's too soon to determine. We've obtained samples of infected blood and tests are being run at Fort Detrick in Maryland to determine all the unknowns. So far, we've had no reported cases of anyone being infected who has not been bit. Once we have anything further, we'll let you know."

The answer only partially calmed Alissa's fears.

"Next question," began Melissa. "With regards to the infected biting their victims, we've heard numerous reports of the infected also eating their victims. Can you comment on this?"

"I can, but I don't have much to tell you. We've also heard reports of victims being eaten and torn apart, but none of them have been confirmed. We're trying to track down the authenticity of such reports because, if true, it could be an indication of what type of virus we're dealing with."

"How so?"

"We could be dealing with a new and highly-virulent form of rabies. Again, let me stress that nothing is certain right now."

The hands went up. SanGiovanni chose a middle-aged man with greying hair and glasses seated at the far end of the second row.

"Mark Bellamah, MSNBC. Given that the virus broke out across the world at approximately the same time, do you think we're experiencing a biological weapons attack?"

"I'm unable to answer that question. You'd have to ask the CIA, the Pentagon, or the FBI. However, in my opinion, considering the outbreak has occurred across the globe and affected every nation, I believe it's naturally occurring."

"Could it be a terrorist organization?"

"I doubt any terrorist organization would have the technology and the resources to develop a weapon so sophisticated and distribute it so precisely. Again, that's a question best answered by the intelligence community."

SanGiovanni pointed to a burly gentleman in the fifth row. "Go ahead."

"Wallace Wayne from SBS World News. If those killed by the infected are coming back to life, do we have to fear that those already dead might also come back?"

SanGiovanni shook her head. "We've received no reports of the previously dead being reanimated, only those who have been killed by the infected. Let me also clarify that the reanimation process is not based on when a person is bitten and infected but on when the person dies. Once an infected person passes on, they reanimate within a few seconds and begin attacking others. We've had—"

An older Asian lady standing off to the side stepped forward and interrupted the doctor.

"What do you mean reanimated? Are you implying that people are being killed in this outbreak and are coming back to life?"

"N-no." SanGiovanni stumbled to correct herself. "That's not what I'm saying."

"But that's what's happening," noted Wayne. "We've had numerous reports from Sydney, Brisbane, and Melbourne of people being attacked, bitten or eaten, and then coming back to life to attack others. You're not getting that here in the States?"

"No," she said, the shock evident in her tone. Most of the other reporters shook their heads and stared at one another, confused.

"Is this true?" asked Bellamah. "Are the victims of these attacks dying and coming back to life?"

SanGiovanni hesitated as all eyes in the auditorium focused on her, waiting her response. She swallowed hard and uttered a single world. "Yes."

Pandemonium broke out at the news conference, with everyone jumping to their feet and shouting questions. Three men emerged from off stage, each wearing dark suits and ties with a microphone draped over their ears. One escorted SanGiovanni off stage, the second escorted the others away, while the third stood behind the podium, shouting over the cacophony of questions.

"This news conference has concluded. We'll let you know when the next one is scheduled."

The camera panned out, showing the chaos that had broken out in the auditorium as reporters in the newsroom commented in the background.

A part of Alissa wanted to finish that bottle of Stolichnaya.

Someone knocking provided welcome relief from the

nightmare playing out on her TV screen. Picking up the Glock and pushing herself off the sofa with a wince, she crossed over to the front door and opened it a crack. Nathan stood on the other side, still in his uniform, and holding a brown paper bag and a Styrofoam holder containing two large drinks.

"May I come in?" he asked, raising the bag and drinks. "I'm bearing gifts."

"You don't need to bring gifts." Alissa opened it all the way. "But if you have food and coffee, I won't complain."

Nathan stepped inside. Being a cop, he immediately noticed the Glock in her hand. "Where did you get that?"

"I took it from a dead State Trooper in the ER."

"Are you serious?"

Alissa frowned.

"Jesus. What the Hell did you go through last night?"

"I'll tell you in a minute." She led the way into the kitchen. "Right now, I'm starving. What do you have?"

"Two sausage, egg, and cheese bagels from the deli and two large coffees, black no sugar. I figured you could add your own."

As Alissa retrieved napkins from the cupboard, Nathan passed out the food and coffee.

"I'm surprised anything is open." Alissa sat down and passed Nathan a few napkins.

"People here are trying to keep things as normal as possible, which isn't easy considering what's going on. The mayor and the chief issued an order last night that if anyone leaves the island, they will not be allowed back." Nathan unwrapped his bagel sandwich and took a bite. "In fact, you were the next to last one allowed through the roadblock."

"I'm lucky." Alissa unwrapped her sandwich. "It's horrible out there. Much worse than the news is reporting."

Nathan took a sip of coffee. "Fill me in."

Alissa spent the next ninety minutes describing in detail everything that had happened to her from the moment she first entered the ER. Nathan listened intently, never once interrupting her, allowing her to vent all the pent-up emotions. Only when she finished, ending the story with falling asleep drunk on the sofa, did he respond.

"I can't believe all you went through. You did good out there."

"I did good?" Alissa had a bitterness in her tone, not toward Nathan but toward herself. "What about all those people I told you about? Do you think I did good by them? I let them all die."

Nathan said nothing. He took the plastic lid off his cup, placed a spoon inside, and stirred the remains of his coffee. "What was the name of those two you left on the roof of the hospital?"

"Courtney and Sophia."

"Why didn't you take them with you?"

"I wanted to, but Courtney knew Sophia would never make it so she decided to stay behind."

Nathan nodded. "And the doctor. Wasn't he dying when you found him?"

"Yes."

"And the patients. Were any of them able to safely make it out of the hospital?"

"No. But—"

Nathan held up his hand. "If any of the Labor and Delivery nurses made it to the lobby with those babies, how far do you think they would have gotten?"

"Not far."

"And those two you met in the pizza shop. Jim…?"

"John and Maria."

"What happened to them?"

"I told you. Maria went back into Boston to save her grandmother."

Nathan stopped stirring, placed the spoon on the table, and sipped. "The teachers and the kids at the school. How long do you think they would have survived outside the building?"

"Enough. I see where—"

"How long?"

"They would have been lucky to last ten minutes."

"I thought you tried to save that cop on the Tobin Bridge."

"He was too heavy for me to pull up."

"But you tried?"

Alissa sighed. "Yes."

"Hmmm." Nathan finished his coffee and replaced the lid. "It sounds to me like you did everything you could for those people."

"How can you say that?"

"Courtney made the decision to stay on the roof and spare Sophia from the nightmare going on inside the hospital. You gave up one of your Glocks, which you needed, to give them a more humane way of ending their lives. The same with that patient you overdosed on morphine."

"What about the other patients?"

"They were not your responsibility. The nurses on that floor abandoned them. They're the ones who must live with their consciences. You couldn't have saved those people in the hospital and the kids at the school."

"I could have tried," Alissa sobbed.

Nathan placed his hand on top of hers and squeezed gently. "You would have gotten them all killed along with yourself. You didn't have to stop and offer them hope. You didn't have to help the nurses in Labor and Delivery, and they decided to make a break that got them killed. I would have done the exact same things you did."

Alissa's mood lightened. "Really?"

"Well, I probably wouldn't have taken the time to put that one patient out of his misery, but you did. Even when the shit hit the fan, you showed a level of humanity most others wouldn't."

Alissa flashed him an awkward smile.

"And you have to stop that shit right now."

The harshness of Nathan's statement caught her off guard. "What do you mean?"

"You have to start looking out for yourself."

"That's not in my nature."

"I know. That's one of the reasons I... that's one of the things that makes you so special. The world fell apart yesterday and the social order collapsed. You have to change the way you think if you want to survive."

Archer jumped up on the table with a loud meow. He circled around the empty wrappers the bagels came in, keeping a wary eye on Nathan. The smell of sausage was too enticing. He inched closer and sniffed the wrapper. A small chunk of meat stuck to a piece of melted cheese clung to the paper. Archer licked it once and, upon finding he liked it, bit down on the glob and dived off the table.

Nathan chuckled. "If you won't do it for yourself, then do it for him."

Alissa smiled. "Thanks. For lunch and the pep talk."

"In my years on the force I've seen a lot of people tear themselves up inside over decisions they made, most of them the best possible decision but with bad consequences. You can't let that happen to you."

"I won't." Alissa patted the top of Nathan's hand. "I promise."

"Good."

A moment of contented silence passed between the two before Nathan said, "I have a question for you. You saw the outbreak up close. How long after a person is bitten before they turn?"

"The determining factor isn't when they were bitten but when they die. Reanimation took place within a few seconds after death."

"You're certain about that?"

"Oh, yeah. The State trooper I worked on had been bitten

a good five to ten minutes before he reached the ER but didn't turn until after he died. The trooper he attacked bled out quickly and then reanimated."

Nathan thought for a moment. "That makes sense."

"What does?"

"The reason they were such assholes at the roadblock last night was the result of an incident that took place earlier. The state set up emergency detention centers for anyone who escaped Boston to make sure that anyone infected did not spread the disease."

"I know. I almost got picked up by one."

"You're lucky you didn't."

Alissa felt a chill race through her body. "Why?"

"Around seven o'clock, one of the detention centers outside of Quincy suffered an outbreak. No one is sure how it started, but within fifteen minutes most of the people in the detention center had turned into deaders. The police wouldn't let the survivors out, so they tore down the gate and made a break for it, releasing the deaders in the process."

"That's horrible."

"It's why the chief is refusing to let anyone on the island who doesn't belong here and is not letting those who leave come back. That all changed this morning. Now no one is allowed in or out."

"Why?"

"A second outbreak occurred in a detention center near Waltham. Same scenario as Quincy, except this time the Guard took no chances and machine gunned everyone in camp, living and living dead."

Alissa gasped. "That's murder."

"That's why we need to get out of here as fast as possible."

"Are you serious?"

"Unfortunately. Sooner or later, either deaders or those seeking safety are going to come down the causeway and we don't have enough manpower to stop either of them. I'm going to take one of the squad cars and get out of here while I can. I'd like you to come with me."

"You really think it's going to get that bad?"

"Yes."

"Then I'm in, as long as I can bring Archer."

"Deal."

"Where are we going?"

"Our best bet is to head as far north as possible where there are few people, maybe the mountains or the coast. I figure we can hole up in a motel for a while and see how the situation develops."

"What about my cabin in New Hampshire?"

"I thought you lost that in the separation."

"Paul and I couldn't agree on who would keep it so we decided to share it rather than spend thousands fighting it out in court. It's available if we need it."

"That'll be perfect. Here's the plan. I'm working from three this afternoon until three in the morning. I'll gather as much intelligence on the situation as I can and see if I can steal any extra weapons and ammo. Pack only the essentials and as many canned goods as you have. I'll swing by at dawn to pick you up. We'll head north and hole up in your cabin until things blow over. Sound like a plan?"

"Do you think we'll get off the island?"

"Getting off won't be a problem. Once we leave, we'll never be allowed back in." Nathan pulled a small notebook from his shirt pocket, jotted down a phone number, then ripped off the page and handed it to Alissa. "This is my cell phone. Call me if you need me. Otherwise I'll see you at dawn."

Alissa escorted Nathan to the front door and opened it. As he left, she gave him a friendly hug. "Thanks. For everything."

"My pleasure. And get a good night's sleep. God knows when we'll have a chance to rest again."

Alissa watched Nathan head down the driveway and get into his squad car, waiting for him to drive off before locking up.

AFTER DRINKING SUCH a huge cup of coffee, Alissa couldn't get any sleep, so she spent the next two hours preparing for their bug out. She removed the cat carrier from the laundry room, which got her several suspicious and angry glares from Archer. Pulling luggage from the top shelf in the garage, she filled two large carry-on bags, one with Archer's cat food, some toys, treats, a spare bowl, and all the medical supplies she had stored in the house, the other with all the canned foods and non-perishables she could find. She placed all three in the front hall. By then it was nearly two in the afternoon, so she decided to go upstairs and get some sleep.

A banging on the front door and the incessant ringing of the bell startled Alissa out of REM sleep. The clock on her nightstand read 3:53. Archer crouched by the stairs, wearily peering down into the front hall. For a few moments she remained groggy until she heard Nathan yelling her name. She bolted up and ran downstairs, whipping open the front door.

"What's wrong?"

"We have to get out of here. Now!"

Chapter Eighteen

ALISSA FELT THAT all-too-familiar adrenalin rush pumping through her body. "Why?"

"The blockade has been breached. Several thousand deaders followed a family trying to escape to Nahant. Let's move."

Alissa pointed to the floor. "Those are packed and ready to go. Give me a minute to get Archer."

"Hurry." Nathan scooped up the bags and headed for the squad car parked out front.

Alissa ran upstairs. Archer lay curled up on the bed. First, she removed the Glock off her nightstand and stuck it between her jeans and the small of her back and slid the remaining magazine in her pocket. Then she picked him up, cuddling and petting him before putting him into the carrier and locking it. "Don't worry, cat. Everything will be all right."

Archer responded with a dissatisfied meow. Alissa made her way downstairs and headed outside, closing the house behind her. She placed the carrier in the back seat of the squad car, secured it with a seat belt, then stood in front of the open passenger side. Nathan talked on his cellphone.

"How are we going to get out if the causeway is blocked?"

"I'm working on that." He held up his hand. "Steve, this is Nathan. Do you still have your boat docked at the Marine Science Center?"

"Yeah. Why?"

"The island is being overwhelmed by deaders and we need a way to escape. Will you help me?"

"Can I bring my family?"

"Of course,"

Alissa waved at Nathan to catch his attention. "They can stay with us in the cabin."

"Steve, Alissa says—"

"I heard. We'll be there in a few minutes."

The other line went dead. Nathan pocketed his cell phone.

A volley of gunfire erupted three streets away followed by screams and the snarls of thousands of deaders. Moments later, an explosion occurred, sending a black cloud of smoke billowing into the air.

"Let's move before others get the same idea I had."

A deader wearing civilian clothes exited from Winter Street a hundred feet ahead and, upon seeing them, charged. Alissa withdrew her Glock, steadied her arms on the top of the open car door, and fired two carefully aimed rounds that blasted away most of its head. The deader's momentum continued driving it forward for a few feet before it toppled over, slamming onto the hood of the squad car and sliding down along the left front fender. The sound of the gunshots attracted other deaders. Three more raced out of Winter Street and rushed them, while another three approached from behind. Alissa raised the Glock and took down one of the deaders to the rear.

"Get in the car," ordered Nathan.

She climbed in and closed the door as Nathan shifted into drive. The car moved forward a few feet and stopped, the left front tire wedged against the civilian-clothed deader. Nathan applied more gas, succeeding only in moving the car a few more inches and digging the tire deeper into the body. The five deaders reached them a second later. One dove onto the hood, hanging on to the upper rim with one hand and slamming the windshield with the other until it cracked. One jumped onto the trunk and clawed at the rear window while the other three went after Alissa, banging against the window. It would not hold up much longer.

Nathan shifted into reverse and pressed his foot on the accelerator. The car backed up and bounced onto the deader corpse behind them. The rear wheels could not get friction on the road, spinning uselessly on top of the body. Nathan kept shifting into drive and reverse, hoping the rocking motion would free the car before the deaders got to them.

Alissa's window shattered and three sets of hands reached in, clutching her hair, face, shoulders, and arms, pulling her toward snapping mouths. She attempted to pull away, but too many hands held her in place. Placing her left palm on the interior of the door and locking it to brace herself. One of the deaders in a leather biker's jacket dug its hand into the back of her neck and used the leverage to pull itself into the car. Its teeth were inches from her cheek, biting frantically. Alissa placed the barrel of the Glock underneath the deader's chin, closed her eyes, and fired three rounds. Inside the confines of the interior, the gunshots were deafening. For a few seconds she couldn't hear anything. However, she felt the remains of the deader's head splash across her face—blood, flesh, teeth, shattered bones. Alissa shook her head, feeling the gore fly off, and opened her eyes. Nothing remained of the deader's head except the rear of its skull dangling from loose skin. The body blocked the window, preventing the other two from gaining access. Alissa used the opportunity. Grabbing the deader by its leather jacket, she held it in place and used it to block the others, taking careful aim and pumping two rounds into the heads of the other two deaders. With the threat gone, Alissa pushed the leather jacket-clad body out of the window.

Nathan continued trying to dislodge the squad car from the body caught beneath, not paying attention to the deader on the hood that continued pounding on the windshield. The glass fractured more with each blow. Alissa aimed the Glock inches from its face. It turned its head toward her and snarled. She fired a single round into its mouth, shattering the windshield outward and blowing the back of the thing's head away.

"Shit!" Nathan swore not because of the unexpected gunshot but because four more deaders slammed into the left side of the car. Their combined weight pushed it far enough to the side that the right rear tire connected with the pavement. The car shot backward and lurched to the left, throwing the deaders across the street and throwing off the one on the trunk, and continued until the rear crashed into a streetlamp. Dozens of deaders closed in on them from the side streets. Nathan shifted into drive and took off, swerving around the closest ones and taking a sharp left onto Winter Street. A pack of deaders blocked their way. He had no time to maneuver, instead pushing the gas pedal to the floor and plowing through them. Four were thrown to the sides. The fifth bounced onto the front of the car, slid across the hood, and smashed into the remains of the windshield. Its head and shoulders broke through. Only the steering wheel stopped it from landing in Nathan's lap. It clawed at him, its fingernails scratching his cheeks. Nathan accelerated.

"Put on your seatbelt!"

Alissa complied. When Nathan heard the click of the belt, he slammed his foot onto the brakes. Alissa lurched forward, the seatbelt preventing her from crashing face-first into the dashboard. Luckily, the momentum had the same effect on the deader. It flew out of the car, across the hood, and hit the street, rolling several times, its dead skin being shredded by the asphalt. As it started to climb to its feet, Nathan gunned the engine. The car slammed into the deader, tossing it to one side.

Nathan paused at Nahant Road. Once again, Alissa found herself in the middle of the outbreak. Terrified civilians and deaders filled the streets. A few hundred feet to the right, five of the remaining volunteers from the roadblock had set up a skirmish line across the road trying to provide cover for those escaping on foot. Deaders flowed over them within seconds, tearing apart the volunteers. The civilians whom they had been protecting only made it a dozen yards before they were also taken down. The remaining deaders extended deeper into the island. A dozen rushed the squad car. Nathan accelerated and turned right, the tires screeching in protest as he swerved around the carnage and made his way to the science center.

Alissa could not believe how rapidly her hometown had devolved into chaos. A dozen cars and minivans raced past them in the opposite direction, trying to escape the island, not realizing they were heading into the horde. Two streets in front of them, a middle-aged woman driving a KIA Sedona jumped the STOP sign on a side street, cutting across Nahant Road and T-boning a family in an Infiniti, sending the latter spinning. The Infiniti crashed into a streetlamp. The middle-aged woman did not even stop to check on them, instead turning onto Nahant Road and heading for the causeway. Hundreds of panicked islanders ran for safety. By now, most had realized that escaping via the causeway was suicide, so they headed for the coast, which merely delayed the inevitable. Nathan avoided those trying to escape, instead plowing through the deaders or those in the process of being eaten.

The chaos dissipated at the edge of town where Nahant Road curved toward the southern shore. By this time, the car limped along on two flat tires and steam drifted from under the hood. The engine made a disturbing knocking noise, although not as loud as Archer who meowed incessantly from his carrier.

"Do you think we'll make it?"

"We should. But we're not far if we do have to walk... We have company."

A teenage girl stood in the center of the street, flagging them down. As Nathan slowed, she ran over to the window, breathing heavily. "Take me with you. Please!"

"Get in."

A deader lunged from behind, knocking the teenager to the ground. Nathan reached for the handle to help her when a second deader rushed up to the window and attempted to climb in.

"Go!" screamed Alissa.

Nathan pulled away from the carnage. When they reached the science center, a chain link security gate blocked the driveway.

"Get down."

Alissa ducked behind the dashboard as Nathan plowed through the barricade. One of the fence's steel supports fell onto the squad car, pushing through the shattered windshield. The fence flew open under the impact, allowing them access. He sped past the science center complex, headed for the dock, and parked near the entrance ramp. Nathan jumped out and threw the carry-on bags over his shoulders.

"You get the cat."

As Alissa pulled the carrier from the back, with Archer protesting with a series of loud and unhappy meows, Nathan opened the trunk and withdrew a large, long bag.

"Are those skis?"

"I raided the police armory for weapons and ammo. We're going to need them."

For a moment, Nathan reminded her of Paul. She owed her ex a huge apology for making fun of his survivalist skills if she ever saw him again.

Nathan rushed down the dock, huffing under the weight he carried. He stopped at a thirty-six-foot cabin cruiser named *Ocean Escape* and dropped the bags onto the back deck. He took the cat carrier from Alissa. "Get in."

Alissa climbed onto the boat and took the carrier from him.

"Stow that stuff in the cabin and stay put."

"Where are you going?"

"To make sure Steve and his family make it."

Alissa brought the carrier inside. She placed it on the kitchen table and went out for the other bags. She could barely lift the one with the guns but managed to get all three inside and dropped them onto a bench by the table. After telling Archer everything would be fine, she headed outside. She couldn't see

Nathan. Jumping off the boat, she ran back to the entrance-way.

Nathan stood by the squad car, nervously checking his watch.

"Where are they?" she asked.

"I thought I told you to stay on the boat?"

"You think I'm some damsel in distress you have to pro-tect?" Alissa withdrew the Glock from her jeans, switched out the empty magazine with a fully loaded one, and held it in both hands. "Screw that shit."

Nathan smiled.

They waited.

After three minutes that felt like an eternity, they heard the roar of a Hemi engine coming down Nahant Road. A minute later, a Ford F-150 pick-up raced around the corner of the science center and sped toward the wharf.

Nathan sighed in relief. "That's Steve and his family."

"And they brought company," added Alissa.

Three hundred feet behind the pick-up, over a hundred deaders rounded the corner of the science center and swarmed toward the wharf.

Chapter Nineteen

"**F**UCK ME," MUMBLED Nathan.

"I think they'd rather eat you." Alissa raised the Glock into firing position. "Let's make sure they choke on their meal."

Steve had enough common sense to swing the Ford around and park it so its rear fender sat inches from the squad car and the front extended over the entranceway to the wharf. It would not stop the deaders, but it might slow them down enough for them all to escape.

The Ford had barely come to a stop when the passenger door opened and a middle-aged woman with long brunette hair jumped out. As Steve slid across the seat, she opened the rear.

"Hurry up," she ordered.

Two children jumped out, a boy approximately eight years old and a girl in her early teens. The mother shoved them towards the wharf. Behind her bossy exterior, Alissa could see terror in the mother's eyes. Steve stepped up to Nathan.

"Sorry I'm late. We almost—"

"No time for that now, buddy. Start the boat. We'll hold them off as long as we can."

Steve followed his family down the wharf as the first of the deaders reached the Ford and thumped into the rear fender.

Alissa recognized it as the asshole who tried to turn her away last night at the blockade. She felt sorry for it. It tried to get at them but could not climb over the rear bed. Other deaders piled up behind it, reaching for the food and snarling. One female deader in fleece pajamas and a bathrobe climbed onto the trunk of the squad car and crawled across. Alissa moved closer. When it looked up and growled, she put a round through its face, blowing off the top of its head from the eyes up. The lower part of its head opened its mouth and snapped its teeth at her.

"I thought head shots were supposed to kill these things," said Alissa as she loaded her last magazine.

Nathan stepped up beside her and fired a second round into the gaping wound, exploding the remainder of its head outward. "Double tap. It works every time."

The pile of deaders grew denser, becoming ten to fifteen bodies deep and extending out to the sides. Those that made it to the front fenders of the two vehicles fell off the parking lot onto the rocky beach, rose back to their feet, and attacked the entranceway to the wharf. It was too high off the ground for them to crawl up. Nathan and Alissa backed away to get out of reach of their hands. The deaders followed them along the sides until they disappeared beneath the surface.

The growing numbers concerned Alissa. None of the deaders could get past the two vehicles, but their combined weight pushed against them, moving them several inches every few seconds.

"We're not going to get out of here alive, are we?"

"Keep the faith," Nathan answered, although his tone did not reflect the same confidence his words did.

The mass pushed the squad car forward a few inches. A thin deader in a jogging outfit squeezed through the narrow gap and, with a ferocious hiss, charged. Nathan aimed and fired off a single round that struck it in the upper jaw. Its mouth blew apart, pieces of flesh-covered jawbone spraying out to the side. The deader collapsed and slid along the wharf for several feet. Other deaders were already trying to push through the gap, their weight moving the squad car further forward.

They had seconds left to live.

Behind them, the engine to *Ocean Escape* roared to life, revving several times. Steve yelled out, "We're ready."

The squad car moved a foot forward and a stream of deaders flowed through the gap, each bearing down on Alissa and Nathan. The two ran for the cabin cruiser, Nathan bringing up the rear, gunning down the closest deaders.

Steve's wife stood on the rear deck, undoing the mooring lines. She waved them on. "Move it. Move it. Move it."

Alissa jumped off the wharf onto the boat, followed a second later by Nathan. As he landed, a dead hand reached up from the water between the wharf and the boat, clasping his ankle. Nathan crashed onto the deck, his weapon flying out of his hand and sliding inside the cabin cruiser. The deader crawled up his leg.

"Let's get out of here!" the wife yelled.

Steve revved the engine. The propeller dug into the deader's lower body, tearing apart its groin. What would be agony for a human barely phased it. It continued pulling itself up Nathan's legs until the propeller blades wrapped around its colon, unwinding the organ. When nothing remained of its insides, the intestines pulled taut, yanking the deader back. However, it still held onto Nathan, dragging him across the deck. Nathan grabbed the bolted chairs on the rear deck. The deader released its grip and disappeared into the water.

Five more deaders ran down the wharf and jumped for the departing boat. Two missed and fell in the cove, sinking beneath the surface. A third bounced off the back deck and ricocheted into the water. The last two landed on the boat. One deader in a bloodied Nahant Police Department uniform dropped to its knees and bent over to bite Nathan's neck. Nathan shoved his forearm under its chin, preventing it from reaching him. The second deader, the teenage girl they tried to rescue earlier, paused, uncertain which prey to go after. Inside the cabin, the two children screamed on seeing the threat. The teenage deader charged them.

Alissa stepped in front of it and raised the Glock, but the thing was too close. It shoved Alissa into the cabin, slamming her against the back of the kitchen bench, knocking the wind out of her. The Glock slid from her hand and fell to the deck. Alissa placed her right palm under its chin and pushed back, holding its head in place. The teenage deader continued lunging, snapping at her extended fingers, and weakening Alissa's grip. The deader closed its mouth around where her pinky met her hand and bit down.

Alissa yelped, expecting to feel teeth dig into flesh, signing her death certificate. Instead, its teeth dug into the bandages, not being strong enough to break skin.

Out of the corner of her eye, Alissa noticed Steve's wife rushing in from the right holding a fire extinguisher like a battering ram. She drove the base into the deader's face. She continued the assault, ramming the extinguisher repeatedly. On the fourth time, the front of its skull fractured and its face caved in. The deader staggered backward, releasing its grip on Alissa.

"Help your friend. I've got this."

Alissa circled behind Steve's wife as she swung the extinguisher around, holding it like a bat and beating the teenage deader over the head. Alissa did not waste time searching for the Glock. Instead, she rushed across the deck and kicked the police deader in the head. The blow did not faze it.

"Here."

Steve's daughter rushed up, holding the Glock by the barrel, and presented it to Alissa.

Alissa took the firearm. "Go back with the others."

As the girl ran into the cabin, Alissa placed the Glock against the top of the deader's head and wrapped her finger around the trigger but did not fire for fear of wounding Nathan.

"Do it," ordered Nathan. "I can't hold it back much longer."

Alissa fired off a single round into the top of the deader's head. Its skull exploded outward, covering the deck, Nathan, and Alissa in blood and brain matter. Nathan raised his right leg, placed his foot against its chest, and kicked. The corpse dropped off the stern and sank beneath the surface. Alissa helped Nathan up.

"Are you okay?"

"I'm fine."

"Were either of you bitten?" The question came from Steve's wife who stood by the entrance to the cabin. She held Nathan's firearm in her left hand, though she kept it by her side, the barrel pointing to the deck. Steve sat at the driver's control off to the left, watching how events played out.

"No," Nathan answered.

"Are you sure?"

"You don't believe us?" asked Alissa.

"I saw that thing bite your hand." She gripped the handle of the firearm.

Nathan glanced over at Alissa. "Is that true?"

"Y-yes," she stuttered. "It didn't break skin. It got me on the bandages."

"Let me see," ordered Steve's wife.

Nathan turned to Alissa. "We'd do the same if one of them might have been bitten."

Resigned to giving in, Alissa crouched down, placed the Glock on the deck, and approached Steve's wife. When Alissa held out her right hand, the woman examined it carefully, turning Alissa's hand over several times. Blood stained the bandages, but it couldn't be determined if it came from a wound or from battle.

"Can you take off the bandages?" Her tone became less harsh. "Please."

Alissa complied, a part of her terrified at what she might find. As the last of the gauze came off, she studied her hand as closely as Steve's wife. A few indentations from the deader's teeth left marks on the skin, but none of them had broken through. Both women sighed in relief.

"I'm so sorry for acting like that."

"No hard feelings. You're only protecting your family."

"Are you sure?"

"Yes."

"Good." The woman hugged Alissa and sniffed back her tears. When she broke the embrace, she held out her hand. "By the way, I'm Miriam."

"Alissa."

"These are our children, Kiera and Little Stevie."

Kiera nodded. Stevie smiled and waved enthusiastically.

"I appreciate you letting us stay with you in New Hampshire."

"It's the least I can do," said Alissa. "You saved our lives."

"And just in time." Nathan pointed to port.

Steve had steered the cabin cruiser along the coast of Nahant about two hundred feet from shore. By the time the battle with the deaders had ended, they had rounded the isolated southern bend and were making their way up the east shore where the death throes of the island played out in gruesome details. All along the coast, humans made desperate attempts at survival. Most ran until they reached a beach or a rocky cliff. Some stopped trying to escape, hugging each other as they waited for death or prayed in their last few moments. Their deaths were brutal but quick. Others fought until the end, using whatever they could find to defend themselves, a gallant yet useless effort that only prolonged the pain. Some ran into the ocean and swam to safety, though she doubted if more than a handful would make it back to the mainland. Even if they did, more deaders would be waiting. Some of those on the rocky cliffs took a chance and dived into the waters below. Almost all were killed or wounded on the stone-strewn coast. Those killed outright were the lucky ones. Deaders followed the flow of jumpers into the surf, those not disabled in the fall crawling over to the wounded and feeding. The screams of the dying could be heard this far out.

The smarter ones made their way to rocky outcrops along the shore. Approximately thirty men, women, and children had climbed the low cliffs of Castle Rock, which extended two hundred feet into the ocean. Deaders packed the base of the cliffs, preventing the humans from escaping. The survivors stood on the edge of the outcrop, waving and shouting to attract the cabin cruiser's attention, which Steve ignored. As the boat passed by, the yelling changed to curses and insults.

"Mom," asked Stevie. "Why don't we save them?"

"Because they're all infected," Nathan lied. "They haven't turned yet."

"So, they're going to die anyways?"

"Yes, honey." Miriam wrapped her arm around the boy and hugged him close.

"I guess it's okay then."

Farther up the coast, a few survivors had swum out to a pair of rock formations protruding from the water two hundred feet from shore called the Spouting Horns. They attempted to wave them down with no success. Two young men dived off the rocks and swam toward the cabin cruiser. Steve steered right and increased speed, pulling away from the two men.

"Are they also infected, mom?"

"Yes." Miriam fought back the tears.

Nathan picked up the travel bag with the canned goods and brought it over to the children. "Hey, guys. Why don't we go below and put the food away? Kiera, could you bring the cat with you?"

"Can we play with him?"

"Of course," said Alissa. "As long as you keep him in one of the cabins."

"Really?" Kiera's eyes brightened.

"Of course."

"What's his name?"

"Archer."

Kiera frowned. "That's not a good name for a cat."

Nathan urged the kids along. "You can give him a nickname later."

The three headed below, with the kids arguing over who would get to pet Archer first. Miriam followed. Alissa took a moment to search for the two men who had been trying to swim out to them but could no longer spot them in the choppy water. She closed her eyes and said a silent prayer for everyone on Nahant, trying not to think of how many more people she could have saved but did not.

Steve leaned back in the driver's chair. "Melissa."

"It's Alissa."

"Sorry. I'm horrible with names."

"That's okay." She joined him. "What do you need?"

"Directions."

Alissa looked back to Nahant with all its surviving inhabitants running to their deaths. She turned away.

"Where do we go now?" asked Steve.

"Any place but here."

"No arguments."

Steve increased speed on the cabin cruiser and headed north.

A Preview of
Nurse Alissa vs. the Zombies II: Escape

ALISSA MADISON STOOD on the stern deck of the cabin cruiser, watching Nahant slowly recede into the distance. In the past thirty-six hours, she had escaped from a deader-ravaged Boston, made her way home through a society falling apart, and now had to evacuate her home when the outbreak spread this far. Fortunately, the combination of distance and the encroaching darkness prevented her from witnessing the death throes of her hometown. Even the screams and cries for help from the islanders had faded, although she wasn't certain if that was because they were too far away to hear them or because everyone had been slaughtered.

A warm, gentle hand touched her shoulder. Miriam, whose husband Steve owned the cabin cruiser, stood behind Alissa. "Is everything okay?"

Will it ever be? Instead of speaking her mind, Alissa muttered, "Yes."

"Steve wants to meet for a few minutes. After that, I'll take you below so you can clean up."

"I appreciate it."

"It's the least I can do. My family is alive because of you and Nathan."

Alissa said nothing as she followed Miriam inside. Nathan stood by the steering compartment with Steve, who sat behind the wheel, guiding the ship. Both men had their attention glued to the radio broadcast coming through the console speaker.

"We have confirmed our earlier report that New Hampshire and

Vermont have closed their southern borders to all traffic. The governors of both states have ordered state and local police, as well as their respective National Guards, to shut down all roads and highways from Massachusetts and New York to prevent the spread of the violence north. According to one State Police representative in Salem, New Hampshire, the use of deadly force has been approved. No one has officially commented on the rumors that the violence has been caused by a highly infectious disease, but one New Hampshire public health worker noted, off the record, that they cannot afford to let rabies spread into the forests because it would be almost impossible to contain. According to unsubstantiated reports we have received, Maine will also seal off their borders within the hour. Stay tuned to this station for further updates."

"My God," Miriam gasped. "It's insane out there."

"I'm afraid it's only going to get worse," Nathan replied.

Steve shook his head in frustration. "We need to get to New Hampshire as soon as possible before they start closing down the waterways."

"Where are the kids?" asked Miriam.

"I sent them downstairs so we could talk in private." Nathan turned to Alissa. "I told them they could play with your cat as long as they weren't rough with him. I hope you don't mind."

"Not at all. Archer is an attention hog. He'll enjoy it."

"Good." Steve paused. "I know we've all been through a lot, but I wanted to plan out tomorrow."

"I thought we were heading for Alissa's cabin?" asked Nathan.

"I don't know where it is."

"It's near North Conway, New Hampshire, not too far from I-93." Alissa thought for a moment. "Sorry, I can't remember the address."

"I don't need that. I need to know the town so I can plot a course."

"Are we heading there now?" Nathan asked.

"It'll be too dangerous to travel at night under these conditions. I plan on anchoring ten miles offshore. We'll head north in the morning."

Miriam grew concerned. "Will we be safe overnight?"

"We should be. Just in case, we'll post a guard. I'll take the first watch until nine. Miriam will go on watch until midnight. Nathan and Alissa can do the next two shifts, and I'll relieve you at six and get us ready to head out. Does that sound fair?"

Everyone agreed.

"Good. Nathan, any chance Miriam and I could borrow one of the weapons you brought on board in case we need to defend ourselves."

"Of course. Any preference?"

"Bring me whatever you can spare as long as it can blast apart the deaders."

"Miriam?"

"I want one." She became embarrassed. "I've never shot one before. What do you recommend?"

Steve and Nathan looked at each other and simultaneously said, "Shotgun."

A spark of excitement lit up Miriam's eyes. "Really?"

Steve chuckled. "My wife's becoming a bad ass."

Miriam leaned over and kissed him. "I thought I already was."

Nathan faced Alissa. "What can I set you up with?"

"I'll take a shotgun as well."

"Are you sure you don't want one of the semi-automatics?"

"I want to make sure I hit what I aim at. Like Miriam, I've never fired anything bigger than a handgun before." A tidal wave of images flooded her memory as she recalled her escape from the hospital and all the deaders she had to shoot. "Until today."

"You got it. I'll get them ready and pass them out later tonight."

Miriam smiled at Nathan and wrapped her hand around Alissa's arm, leading her below. "We need to get you a hot shower and a change of clothes."

"I didn't bring any with me."

"Don't worry about that. I can lend you some of mine. My husband says I have too much anyways."

MIRIAM SHOWED ALISSA to her cabin, pulled a facecloth and several towels from the linen closet, and told Alissa she could take whatever clothes she wanted from her wardrobe. Once Miriam had left, Alissa stripped out of her soiled outfit and placed it on the tiled floor in the bathroom. The blood had soaked through to her underwear, so she added them to the pile. She also removed the bandages around her right pinky and waist, leaving them on the counter. A minute later, hot water streamed over her face and down her body. Only this time Alissa did not use the shower to relax and wind down, merely to clean herself. It was too painful to twist and bend due to the bruise on her left side. Once she had rinsed away all the blood, she dried off and re-entered the state room.

Archer sat on the bed with his legs folded under him. Upon seeing his mistress, he meowed once and rolled onto his back, stretching out his legs and exposing his belly. Alissa sat on the bed and slid her right hand across his stomach, massaging his chin with her thumb and forefinger. Archer allowed himself the simple pleasure for a few seconds before wrapping his front paws around her wrist. He gently bit her hand while kicking at her arm with his hind legs, an affectionate gesture on his part. After a minute, Archer let go, rolled onto his paws, and rushed onto the pillows where he proceeded to groom himself.

"I love you, too, asshat."

Alissa watched Archer, happy that, despite everything, she had saved him. He had been her sole source of comfort since Paul had asked for a separation twelve months ago. Losing Archer would have devastated her. For the first time, she began to realize how lucky she had been. So many families had lost loved ones or were completely devastated by the spread of this virus. Sure, Alissa had gone through her own Hell and had lost her home, yet everything truly important to her had survived. Once they made their way to her cabin, with luck they could ride out this crisis and be able to begin their lives over.

Alissa returned to the bathroom and checked her wounds. The pinky still hurt from where she had dislocated it on the scaffolding while trying to escape from the hospital, but it had full mobility. The skin under the ribcage under her left arm was heavily bruised, a black and blue nearly a foot long and six inches wide, having nearly doubled from the day before. She winced when she pressed against it, the area still being extremely tender. All she needed were pain killers and a few weeks to rest, the latter of which she doubted she would get. Searching through the cabinets, Alissa could not find any new bandages. No big deal. The original ones were still relatively clean. She wrapped the longest gauze tightly around her chest and then shifted to her pinky, reusing the makeshift splint she had made from an old emery board.

Returning to the stateroom, Alissa opened the closet. She slipped on the panties Miriam had given her. The bra, however, was much too big. No problem. She could go without one until they reached the cabin. No one would be paying attention one way or the other. Sorting through the clothes in the closet, she eventually picked out a pair of jeans and a white sweater that were comfortable and durable enough for what lay ahead. She draped the clothes over the back of a chair and prepared to go to bed, then thought about it. Things went south quickly back on Nahant and she and Nathan had only minutes to get to safety. She would hate to have to face another emergency while naked. She pulled on the clothes she had picked out and slid under the covers. The sway of the ship along the waves relaxed Alissa, who feel asleep within minutes.

The last thing she remembered before dozing off was Archer curling up in a ball against the back of her head and purring contentedly.

A Thank You to My Readers

I love telling stories. I have since I was a kid. The best part is having people who listen to and enjoy them. I'm very fortunate that I get to relate some dark, bizarre, and demented tales and have a fanbase that devours them like zombies eating human flesh. You keep reading and I'll keep writing.

If you liked *Nurse Alissa vs. the Zombies*, please post a review on Amazon. The review does not have to be long—just a rating and a sentence or two about why you enjoyed it. The more reviews *Nurse Alissa vs. the Zombies* receives, the more opportunity other readers have of discovering the book.

The *Nurse Alissa* saga will continue. Over the next few books, Alissa and the other survivors will face even more deaders, meet human friends and enemies, and encounter situations that make the outbreak seem tame by comparison. There are even plans for a spin-off series that will take the deader outbreak to new and fun levels. I can't promise that your favorite characters will survive but I can promise some good gut munching, zombie slaying, gore-filled action.

Acknowledgments

I say this in all my books, but it's true. Writing is very solitary and lonely but getting a book published is a complicated process involving many people, all of whom deserve to be recognized. No writer can be successful without help.

A major thanks goes out to my beta readers: Tammy Michelle Mayberry, Michael Atkinson, Pammy Troupe, Tom Williamson, Marla Dewitt, Dan Uebel, Norma Seitz, Roseann Powell, and Cari Laffrenier Thompson.

Christian Bentulan designed the cover art for this novel.

You would not be holding this book were it not for my dear friend and colleague Alina Ionescu. I hadn't written a zombie series since *Rotter Apocalypse* was published in 2015. Alina is a major fan of my zombie stories and kept urging me to go back to writing about the living dead. With some gentle shoving in the right direction and a few well-placed ideas, over the course of a long week on the road I came up with the concept of the Alissa series. If you like this series, thank Alina.

Finally, a major debt of thanks goes to my family, human and furry. It's hard to maintain my writing discipline. I have a demilitarized zone in my house to keep the cats and dogs separated because by Boxer Bella hates Archer (yes, the Archer in the novel is based on my real cat, who I also call Asshat). Plus, being a stay-at-home dad is not as an ideal life as everyone might think. However, my family gives me the time I need to write, albeit sometimes reluctantly, and never holds my self-imposed isolation against me. I couldn't do this without their love and support.

About the Author

Scott M. Baker was born and raised in Everett, Massachusetts and spent twenty-three years in northern Virginia working for the Central Intelligence Agency. Scott is now retired and lives just outside of Concord, New Hampshire with his wife and fellow writer Alison Beightol, stepdaughter, two rambunctious boxers, and two cats who treat him as their human servant. He has written *Shattered World I: Paris* and *Shattered World II: Russia*, the first two books in his five-book young adult post-apocalypse series about a group of adventurers attempting to close portals into Hell; *The Vampire Hunters* trilogy, about humans fighting the undead in Washington D.C.; *Rotter World, Rotter Nation,* and *Rotter Apocalypse*, his post-apocalyptic zombie saga; *Yeitso*, his homage to the giant monster movies of the 1950s that he loved watching as a kid; as well as several zombie-themed novellas and anthologies.

Please check out Scott's social media accounts for the latest information on future books, upcoming events, and other fun stuff.

Blog: scottmbakerauthor.blogspot.com
Facebook: facebook.com/groups/397749347486177
Twitter: twitter.com/vampire_hunters
Instagram: instagram.com/scottmbakerwriter